TANG POEMS
IN ORIGINAL RHYME

原韻英譯唐詩精選

Translated by C. K. Ho

何中堅 譯

商務印書館

Tang Poems in Original Rhyme
原韻英譯唐詩精選

選譯：何中堅
Selected and translated by：C. K. Ho
責任編輯：黃家麗
Executive Editor：K. L. Wong
出版：商務印書館（香港）有限公司
Published by：The Commercial Press (H.K.) Limited
香港筲箕灣耀興道3號東滙廣場8樓
8/F, Eastern Central Plaza,
3 Yiu Hing Road, Shau Kei Wan, Hong Kong
http://www.commercialpress.com.hk

發行：香港聯合書刊物流有限公司
Distributed by：The SUP Publishing Logistics (H.K.) Limited
香港新界大埔汀麗路36號中華商務印刷大廈3字樓
3/F, C&C Building, 36 Ting Lai Road,
Tai Po, N. T., Hong Kong

印刷：中華商務彩色印刷有限公司
Printed by：C&C Offset Printing Co., Ltd.
香港新界大埔汀麗路 36 號中華商務印刷大廈 14 字樓
14/F, C&C Building, 36 Ting Lai Road,
Tai Po, N. T., Hong Kong

版次：2018 年 6 月第 1 版第 2 次印刷
Edition：First Edition, Second Printing, June 2018
© 2015 商務印書館（香港）有限公司
ISBN 978 962 07 0396 6

獻給我的母親陳淑佳
Dedicated to My Mother Chan Sook Kai

樹欲靜而風不息。　　　　子欲養而親不在。
A tree wants peace,　　　　*A son wants to repay,*
But the wind won't cease.　*But his parents won't stay.*

Contents
目　錄

TANG POEMS　唐詩

APPENDIX　附錄

SONG POEMS　宋詩

TANG & SONG LYRICS　唐宋詞

Preface

In this incredible brainchild of Mr. C.K. Ho, you will find English translations of Tang Poems (唐詩) that straightly adhere to the unique *Ho Translation Style* – recreating the melodic beauty of rhyme and rhythm of ancient Chinese poems in simple English without compromising translation accuracy. To practice the Ho Translation Style requires a deep understanding of Chinese literature and a high level of proficiency in both English and Chinese. Each translated poem is not only a brilliant piece of literature in its own right, but also a tool that helps bridge the cultural and linguistic barriers for English-speaking readers who are not proficient in Chinese so that they can better appreciate the poems. The book should help popularize Tang Poems internationally.

This book is full of pleasant surprises. There are many examples of clever and elegant translations of the ancient Chinese language using simple English. This book also provides an enjoyable way for Chinese readers to improve their command of English. It is suitable for a wide range of readers. For younger ethnic Chinese who study in English-speaking environments (such as international schools or abroad) but are interested in or curious about Tang Poems, this is an excellent introductory book. For those who are familiar with Tang poetry, they can appreciate the beauty of the Ho Translation Style, which, I believe, will be studied by serious academics in the future.

This book should also serve as a good reference for students and scholars in translation, comparative literature, and Chinese literature.

Professor K. W. Chau
The University of Hong Kong

前言

　　讀者會發現，本書內的英譯唐詩，完全按照譯者自己所創的獨特手法譯出。其獨特及令人難以置信之處，在於竟然能夠以淺白的英語，重塑古詩優雅悦耳的韻律及節奏，而不損翻譯的準確性，因而別具風格。此種風格，我稱之為**"何氏翻譯風格"**。要實踐"何氏翻譯風格"，譯者必須對中國文學有深入認識及精通中英兩種語文。書中每篇英譯唐詩不僅本身就是出色的文學作品，而且可以作為貫通中外文化及語言的橋樑，讓不精通中文的外國人也可以欣賞唐詩，從而促進在國際上推廣唐詩。

　　本書內充滿教人驚歎及喜出望外的例子。譯者巧妙地，用淺白的英語，將古文翻譯為優美的英語詩篇。因此，本書可以使到讀者在享受閱讀樂趣之餘，提升英語水平。本書亦適合於各種各類的讀者。對於年青的、在英語環境成長的一代（譬如就讀於國際學校或留學外國），而對唐詩抱有興趣或好奇心者，本書是極佳的入門讀本。至於對唐詩有所認識者，他們將會欣賞此種創新的翻譯風格美妙之處。本人相信"何氏翻譯風格"，日後定必為處事認真的學者所探討。

　　除此之外，對就讀於翻譯、比較文學及中國文學的學生，及從事相關研究的學者來說，這本書同時亦是上佳的參考材料。

鄒廣榮教授
香港大學

Translator's Preface

Poems of the Tang Dynasty (A.D. 618 – A.D. 907) are succinct and beautiful. They have been popular among the Chinese people all over the world for over 1,400 years. Many of these are real masterpieces containing phrases that have since become proverbial in the Chinese language.

An innovative approach was adopted to reproduce 202 most popular Tang poems in English by preserving their compelling qualities while faithfully recreating the text. The translations in this book are unique in that they rhyme in the same way as the originals. My aim is to make the translated versions elegant and melodious like the originals. Simple English is used to ensure pleasant reading.

Tang poems rhyme in a way very different from English poems. A single rhyme often runs through an entire poem. Generally the same rhyme is repeated between two to five times in a poem. Sometimes a rhyme is repeated up to seven or eight times or more in Gu Poems (古詩). In Du Fu's 'To Mr Wei, the Eighth' (杜甫贈衛八處士), the same rhyme is repeated twelve times. Good rhyming gives Tang poems superb musical quality. They are therefore pleasant to read, to recite and to hear.

I note with disappointment that many Tang poems have been translated into line by line prose bearing little resemblance to the originals. Rhyming is either absent or imposed in pairs at the expense of meaning. Such translations do not reproduce the beauty of Tang poems. I believe the beauty of Tang poems may only be reproduced in English if the qualities that made them beautiful are successfully preserved.

I was prompted to embark on the translation by my love for Chinese literature and my desire to show to the world, especially to the younger generation, the beauty of Tang poems.

Young people are often put off by difficult classical words in Tang poems, especially by allusions and metaphors. An easy-to-understand English version may arouse their interest in traditional Chinese culture. To help readers better understand and appreciate the poems, footnotes are included after some poems to explain an allusion, a metaphor, a tradition, a place or the background.

Translating classical Chinese poems into English is a challenging task. Due to the enormous difference between the two languages and the cultures of the two peoples, there are many limitations and obstacles. Over the past six years, much time and effort was spent on research on the background and brain searching for suitable words to be used for a poem or even a single line. The most difficult part was in the choice of words and phrases that would serve the purpose while at the same time preserving the rhyme, rhythm, soul, flavour and format of the original poems.

The following is an example of rhyme and rhythm matching:

To thirty thousand feet
my white hair would grow,
'Cause like this long is my woe.

There's autumn frost
in the bright mirror –
From where it came I hardly know.
('Songs by the Riverbank No.15' by Li Bai)

白髮三千丈，緣愁似箇長。
不知明鏡裏，何處得秋霜。

Balance and antithesis (對仗) is often present in classical Chinese poetry. It enhances the vividness of the pictures presented before the reader. I have attempted to match this in English as far as possible so that the lines would be as lively and impressive as the originals. The following is an example of balance and antithesis matching:

Hard it was to meet you —
  hard as well to say goodbye.
The east wind's powerless, all flowers die.

Only when a spring silk-worm perishes,
  would its silk be exhausted;
Only when a candle burns to ashes,
  would its tears dry.

(Excerpt from 'Untitled (1)' by Li Shangyin)

相見時難別亦難，東風無力百花殘。
春蠶到死絲方盡，蠟炬成灰淚始乾。

An Appendix containing two Song poems (宋詩) and six Tang and Song lyrics (唐宋詞) are included at the end of the book. I hope readers will equally enjoy reading these after reading the 202 Tang poems.

My heart-felt thanks are due to my colleagues and friends at The University of Hong Kong for their support of my work, particularly to Professor K. W. Chau and Mr. H. F. Leung. A very special thanks is due to C. T. who patiently and critically read the entire manuscript and gave me invaluable opinions and suggestions continuously over the past six years.

I would also like to express my profound gratitude to Miss Betty K. L. Wong of The Commercial Press (H.K.) Ltd. for her excellent editorial work and advice over the long years of preparation of this volume.

C. K. Ho

譯者前言

　　唐詩簡潔而華麗。自唐朝(公元 618 — 公元 907)迄今，唐詩傳誦於國內及海外華人社會凡一千四百餘年。其中很多是家傳戶曉的偉大名作。詩篇內亦有不少大家耳熟能詳的名句及成語。

　　本人採用完全創新手法，以英語重塑二百零二首家傳戶曉的唐詩。既保留其優美動人的特質，又忠實地譯出其原意。此英譯本獨特之處，在於英譯詩篇與原詩以同樣方式押韻，令英譯本如同原詩一樣優美及富音樂感。譯本採用簡單英語，以求唸起來流暢自然。

　　唐詩的押韻方式與英詩很不同。唐詩全詩用同一個腳韻，亦即所謂"一韻到底"。一般來説，在一首詩內，同一腳韻用兩三次(如絕句)或四五次(如律詩)。在古詩及樂府詩，一韻可能用七八次以上。在杜甫的"贈衛八處士"詩內，同一個腳韻用上十二次之多。 唐詩韻律豐富和諧，有極佳音樂感，因此無論是讀、吟或聽起來都教人覺得舒服。

　　很可惜，坊間所見之唐詩英譯本，皆以散文短句平鋪直譯，與原詩樣貌不同，而且並不押韻。偶有配以"對韻"，卻往往為求配韻而扭曲詩句原意。 如此一來，當然不能重塑唐詩之美。我認為必須在翻譯過程中，成功保留其各種優美動人的特質，才能活現原詩神韻。

　　我從事此項創新翻譯，是因為我對中國文學的熱愛，以及我渴望向全世界 —— 特別是年青一代 —— 展示唐詩美妙傳神之處。

　　現在的年輕人往往被唐詩內艱深的詞語、隱喻、典故嚇怕，這些艱深部份，我已在一些詩的下面加上腳註，也補充説明了傳説風俗及當時的歷史背景，以幫助讀者欣賞唐詩，這樣一個淺白易明，譯法創新的英譯本，很可能會引起年輕人對傳統中華文化的興趣。

　　將古典詩詞翻譯成英語是一項極具挑戰性的工作。中國人和外國人無論在語言或文化上都存在巨大差異。因此，我在翻譯過程中遇上相當多困難和障礙 。很多時要花許多時間精力鑽研一首甚或一句詩的背境及典故，或是絞盡腦汁來選詞用字。最困難的是尋找合適字詞，而這些字詞必須同時能夠保留原詩的意思、韻律、節奏、神髓及格調。

　　以下是一則用英語配韻及節奏的例子：

　　　白髮三千丈，緣愁似箇長。
　　　不知明鏡裏，何處得秋霜。

（李白〔秋浦歌十七首其十五〕詩）

　　　To thirty thousand feet
　　　　　my white hair would grow,
　　　'Cause like this long is my woe.

　　　There's autumn frost
　　　　　in the bright mirror —
　　　From where it came I hardly know.

　　古代詩人經常用"對仗"手法加強詩句的感染力，令場景及詩意活現讀者眼前。 翻譯時我亦盡量用英語重塑"對仗"，以求翻譯出來的詩句，同樣生動而富有感染力。

　　以下是一則用英語"對仗"的例子：

　　　相見時難別亦難，東風無力百花殘。
　　　春蠶到死絲方盡，蠟炬成灰淚始乾。

（節錄自李商隱〔無題〕詩）

Hard it was to meet you –
  hard as well to say goodbye.
The east wind's powerless, all flowers die.

Only when a spring silk-worm perishes,
  would its silk be exhausted;
Only when a candle burns to ashes,
  would its tears dry.

　　書後附錄選收了兩首英譯宋詩及六首英譯唐宋詞。但願讀者看了這二百零二首英譯唐詩後，同樣喜歡欣賞這幾首美妙動人的宋詩及唐宋詞。

　　衷心感謝香港大學的同事及友好，在這六年來的支持，尤其是鄒廣榮教授及梁慶豐先生。另外特別要感謝 C. T. 這些年來耐心認真地審閱全部文稿，及提出不少寶貴意見。

　　最後亦要衷心感謝香港商務印書館的黃家麗小姐在籌備本書當中給予我的指點、協助及其精湛的編輯技巧。

何中堅

TANG POEMS
唐詩

A TRAVELLER'S SONG

Meng Jiao (751 — 814)

Threads in an affectionate mother's hands
Are clothes on a son who's going away.

Finer and finer she puts
　　her stitches before he leaves,
For fear his return may run into long delay.

Our heart, tiny as an inch-long blade of grass,
Who says the sunshine of spring[1] it can repay?

遊子吟

孟郊（751 — 814）

慈母手中線，
遊子身上衣。

臨行密密縫，
意恐遲遲歸。

誰言寸草心，
報得三春暉。

---

1 This is a metaphor. The sunshine of spring to a blade of grass is like motherly love to a son that can never be adequately repaid.

NIGHT VIEW ON A BRIDGE IN LUOYANG

Meng Jiao (751 — 814)

洛橋晚望

孟郊（751 — 814）

New ice is formed
    the Tianjin Bridge[1] below:
On the footpaths of Luoyang,
    not a single man would show.

Elms and willows look thin,
    houses desolate;
In the bright moonlight,
clearly seen is Mt Song's[2] snow.

天津橋下冰初結，
洛陽陌上行人絕。

榆柳蕭疏樓閣閒，
月明直見嵩山雪。

1　An ancient bridge in the city of Luoyang in Henan Province.
2　One of the five large mountains of China (五嶽之一). It is in Henan Province.

UPON PASSING THE STATE EXAMINATION

Meng Jiao (751 — 814)

登科後

孟郊（751 — 814）

My humble past
　　isn't worth boasting in any way,
But I'm unrestrained
　　and full of inspiration today.

Riding high in the spring breeze,
　　off I go at full gallop,
To view all the flowers
　　of Chang'an[1] in one day.

往日齷齪不堪誇，
今朝放蕩思無涯。

春風得意馬蹄疾，
一日看盡長安花。

1　The capital in Tang Dynasty. It is now the city of Xi'an.

Background:
This poem was written immediately after the poet knew of his success in the State Examination and was filled with exaltation. He failed twice in the past.

ON THE WEST OF LONG MOUNTAIN[1]

Chen Tao (812 — 855)

By death they swore,
      to send the Huns[2] to hell;
On barbarian soil,
      five thousand warriors in sables[3] fell.

How sad their bones are lying by
      the Wu-ding River[4]:
In the spring dreams of many wives,
      their spirits still dwell.

---

1 Long Mountain （隴山） is situated in Gansu Province.
2 Also known as Xiongnu. These were barbarians who from time to time raided the Chinese towns along the ancient northern border.
3 Elite warriors wore sable furs in winter in the northwest frontier.
4 A river on the northwest border.

隴西行

陳陶 (812 — 885)

誓掃匈奴不顧身，
五千貂錦喪胡塵。

可憐無定河邊骨，
猶是春閨夢裏人。

OLD STYLE POEMS (1)
(Have Pity on the Farmers)

Li Shen (772 — 846)

古風二首 （1）
（憫農）

李紳 (772 — 846)

A millet one sows in spring,
Ten thousand grains
    one harvests in autumn thereby.

No fields lie fallow in the whole world:
Still, of hunger farmers die.

春種一粒粟，
秋收萬顆子。

四海無閒田，
農夫猶餓死。

Background:
This poem reflected the lamentable situation of farmers who worked hard but were sometimes starved to death due to heavy taxes in ancient times.

OLD STYLE POEMS (2)
(Have Pity on the Farmers)

Li Shen (772 — 846)

古風二首 （2）
（憫農）

李紳 （772 — 846）

Hoeing the crops in the midday sun,
Sweat drips to the soil.

Who knows that of our meal in the dish,
Every grain comes after hard toil?

鋤禾日當午，
汗滴禾下土。

誰知盤中餐，
粒粒皆辛苦。

MOORING BY THE MAPLE BRIDGE AT NIGHT

Zhang Ji (around 750)

楓橋夜泊

張繼（大約 750 年）

The moon's setting amid the caws of crows,
　　the sky frosted over in whole;
Fronting riverside maples
　　and fishing fires[1] lies a sad soul.

The Cold Mountain Temple
　　is outside the Gusu City[2] –
To the guest boat comes its midnight toll.

月落烏啼霜滿天，
江楓漁火對愁眠。

姑蘇城外寒山寺，
夜半鐘聲到客船。

1　Fishermen in the old days lit fires when they fished at night time to lure fish into the net.

2　The old name of Suzhou City in Zhejiang Province.

Background:
The poet fled his home during the An Lushan Rebellion (安史之亂 A.D.755 — A.D.763). He spent a night in a boat by a river in Suzhou City while he was on his way to Central Wu (吳中) in today's Zhejiang Province. Worrying about his war-torn country, he felt sad and had a sleepless night.

AT THE CITY TOWER GATE OF WU [1]

Zhang Ji (around 750)

吳門即事

張繼 (約 750 年)

With farmer-conscripts [2],
    one by one off the multi-decked ships go;
In the boundless rice fields,
    green, green grasses of spring grow.

Try climbing up the tower gate
    to look outside the city –
It's already Qing Ming but
    how many new smokes would show [3]?

耕夫召募逐樓船，
春草青青萬頃田。

試上吳門看郡郭，
清明幾處有新煙？

---

1 The county of Wu in Suzhou City.

2 Farmers were often conscripted and sent to battlefields in ancient times. Large multi-decked ships were used for the purpose.

3 As a rule, people would start lighting fires and resumed cooking at Qing Ming Festival after the Cold Food Festival during which lighting fires was not allowed. The poet hinted that few people were lighting fires as few had rice to cook (i.e. many were starving) because many rice fields were deserted and overgrown with grass after the farmers were conscripted.

RETURNING HOME

He Zhizhang (659 — 744)

I left home young but on return old I became;
The hair on my temples turned grey
　　　but my accent remained the same.

Children greeted me but knew me not:
With a giggle, they asked from where I came.

回鄉偶書

賀知章（659 — 744）

少小離家老大回，
鄉音無改鬢毛衰。

兒童相見不相識，
笑問客從何處來。

DRINKING ALONE
UNDER THE MOON

Li Bai (701 — 762)

月下獨酌

李白 (701 — 762)

With a jug of wine among flowers,
Alone I drink, unaccompanied
  by anyone I know.

I raise my cup to invite the bright moon:
Including my shadow, a party of three I throw.

The moon knows not the pleasure of drinking;
My shadow vainly follows me wherever I go.

The moon and shadow
  are for now my companions:
Let's enjoy life while our young hearts glow.

As I sing, the moon lingers around;
As I dance, my shadow moves in disarray.

When I'm sober, together we make merry;
When I'm drunk, separate we stay.

Let's pledge forever to be
  passionless roaming partners,
To meet again in the faraway Milky Way.

花間一壺酒，
獨酌無相親。

舉杯邀明月，
對影成三人。

月既不解飲，
影徒隨我身。

暫伴月將影，
行樂須及春。

我歌月徘徊，
我舞影零亂。

醒時同交歡，
醉後各分散。

永結無情遊，
相期邈雲漢。

17 SONGS BY THE RIVERBANK IN AUTUMN (No.15)

Li Bai (701 — 762)

秋浦歌十七首
（其十五）

李白（701 — 762）

To thirty thousand feet
    my white hair would grow,
'Cause like this long is my woe.

There's autumn frost
    in the bright mirror –
From where it came I hardly know.

白髮三千丈，
緣愁似箇長。

不知明鏡裏，
何處得秋霜。

FAREWELL PARTY AT JINLING [1]

Li Bai (701 — 762)

金陵酒肆留別

李白（701 — 762）

Willow flowers flying in the wind
    fill the tavern with sweet scent;
To the guests, newly brewed wine
    the Wu [2] waitresses ardently present.

Come the youngsters of Jinling [1] to see me off,
We linger and drink to our hearts' content.

Please try to ask the east-flowing river
    which one would last longer:
Its water or our parting sentiment?

風吹柳花滿店香，
吳姬壓酒勸客嚐。

金陵子弟來相送，
欲行不行各盡觴。

請君試問東流水，
別意與之誰短長。

---

1 Former name of the city of Nanjing.
2 The area around Jiangsu Province was generally referred to as Wu in ancient times, being the former
   domain of the kingdom of Wu (A.D. 220 — A.D. 280).

Ascending the Phoenix Terrace at Jinling[1]

Li Bai (701 — 762)

登金陵鳳凰臺

李白 (701 — 762)

Phoenixes once roamed
　　on the Phoenix Terrace ground.
They're gone: the Terrace's empty,
　　the river keeps rolling on unbound.

Solitary paths of the Wu[2] Palace
　　lie buried under flowers and weeds;
Aristocrats of Jin[2] in the ancient mound.

The three peaks[3]
　　rise halfway into the blue sky;
The two rivers[4]
　　split where the Egret Isle is found.

The sun can be darkened with clouds:
Losing sight of Chang An[5] makes me feel down.

鳳凰臺上鳳凰遊
鳳去臺空江自流

吳宮花草埋幽徑
晉代衣冠成古丘

三山半落青天外
二水中分白鷺洲

總為浮雲能蔽日
長安不見使人愁

1　Former name of the city of Nanjing.
2　Both the Wu and Jin Dynasties had their capitals in Nanjing.
3　A large mountain called "Sam-shan" meaning literally "three peaks" along the Yangtze River on southwest of the city of Nanjing.
4　The Qinhuai River meets the Yangtze River in Nanjing where they split around the Egret Isles.
5　The capital in Tang Dynasty, it is now the city of Xi'an.

Background:
Li Bai was not in the capit
He expressed his sadness
the end of the poem for n
being able to contribute
his country during a peri
of turbulence. He could n
see the capital Chang'an fr
where he stood and the clou
surrounding the sun made h
worry that the Emperor cou
be surrounded by medioc
ministers.

SAILING DOWN TO JIANGLING

Li Bai (701 — 762)

白帝下江陵

李白（701 — 762）

Bai Di[1] we left
　　under rosy clouds at dawn;
To Jiang Ling[2] we returned in
　　a day's journey a thousand miles long.

Amidst incessant howling
　　of gibbons on the shores,
Through myriads of mountains
　　our light boat had gone.

朝辭白帝彩雲間，
千里江陵一日還。

兩岸猿聲啼不絕，
輕舟已過萬重山。

1 A town along the Yangtze
　River near the Three Gorges
　in Sichuan Province.
2 A town along the Yangtze
　River in Hubei Province.

MY VIEW ON LIFE UPON WAKING UP FROM A DRUNKEN SLUMBER IN SPRING

Li Bai (701 — 762)

春日醉起言志

李白（701 — 762）

Life's like a big dream:
People toil throughout – but why?

處世若大夢，
胡為勞其生。

I'd therefore get drunk all day –
Disheartened, by the front pillar I'd lie.

所以終日醉，
頹然臥前楹。

Waken, I see in the front courtyard
A bird amid the flowers cry.

覺來盼前庭，
一鳥花間鳴。

Tell me what day this is –
Now spring breezes
    chatter with orioles passing by.

借問此何日，
春風語流鶯。

Another cup of wine I pour
But overwhelmed, I all but sigh.

感之欲嘆息，
對酒還自傾。

Aloud I sing expecting the bright moon …
    When the song ends, the theme forget I.

浩歌待明月，
曲盡已忘情。

NIGHT THOUGHTS

Li Bai (701 — 762)

The bright moon shines before my bed:
I wonder if it's frost on the ground spread.

At the bright moon I look up,
And yearn for my old home as I lower my head.

夜思

李白（701 — 762）

牀前明月光，
疑是地上霜。

舉頭望明月，
低頭思故鄉。

LET'S DRINK

Li Bai (701 — 762)

Don't you see,
The water of the Yellow River
    from Heaven is brought –
To the sea it rushes and returns not?

Don't you see,
By the mirror over their white hair
    our parents grieve –
It's like black silk in the morn but snow at eve?

Make merry to the full
    when life's wishes are granted;
Under the moon,
    gold jugs unattended one mustn't leave.

I'm endowed with talents
    that must be put to use;
A thousand pieces of gold squandered –
    but return they would, the whole lot.

Cook a lamb, slay an ox and be happy:
To drink three hundred cups we ought!

Master Cen[1], Mr Danqiu[2],
Let's drink! Put down not your wine.

將進酒

李白（701 — 762）

君不見，
黃河之水天上來，
奔流到海不復回？

君不見，
高堂明鏡悲白髮，
朝如青絲暮成雪？
人生得意須盡歡，莫使金樽空對月。

天生我材必有用，千金散盡還復來。
烹羊宰牛且為樂，會須一飲三百杯。

岑夫子，丹丘生，
將進酒，杯莫停。
與君歌一曲，請君為我傾耳聽：

鐘鼓饌玉不足貴，但願長醉不願醒。
古來聖賢皆寂寞，惟有飲者留其名。

陳王昔時宴平樂，斗酒十千恣歡謔。
主人何為言少錢？逕須沽取對君酌。

五花馬，千金裘，
呼兒將出換美酒，與爾同銷萬古愁。

LET'S DRINK (Cont'd)

Li Bai (701 — 762)

For you I'd sing –
Please lend me your ears to this song of mine:

Sumptuous feasts with music I prize little,
I only wish I were forever drunk
     and regain not a conscious mind.

Saints and sages from of old
     passed away unnoticed:
Only drinkers left their names behind.

Feast at Pingle[3] the King of Chen[4] used to:
Wine costing ten thousand coins a pint
     they enjoyed through and through.

How can a host say money he lacks?
Wine he should buy to drink with you.

Take the five-colour dappled horse –
     the priceless mink to follow.

My son I'd call to trade them for fine wine:
Together we'll drink away our endless sorrow!

1 A poet and good friend of Li Bai named Cen Shen.

2 A Taoist recluse named Yuan Danqiu.

3 Pingle Palace.

4 Cao Zhi (曹植), son of Cao Cao (曹操) and King of the State of Chan in the Three Kingdoms Period (A.D. 220 – A.D. 280).

Background:
Li Bai was very fond of drinking. This poem reflected the real reason why he indulged in drinking. He was talented and ambitious to serve his country. However, luck was never on his side and his ambition could not be fulfilled as he wished. He was unhappy and resorted to drinking so as to 'drink away' his endless sorrow as he put it in the last line of this poem.

LU SHAN WATERFALL

Li Bai (701 — 762)

The sun shines upon the Censer Peak
    where purple mist begins to rise;
A waterfall in the distance
    hangs over the river before my eyes.

Down three thousand feet
    its pouring water hurtles:
I wonder if it's the Milky Way
    fallen from the nine skies[1].

望廬山瀑布

李白（701 — 762）

日照香爐生紫煙，
遙看瀑布掛前川。

飛流直下三千尺，
疑是銀河落九天。

---

1 In ancient China, people thought there were nine skies above them.

THE MOON OVER THE MOUNTAIN PASS

Li Bai (701 — 762)

關山月

李白 (701 — 762)

The bright moon emerges
    from behind Tian Shan[1],
Amidst a sea of clouds boundless in its span.

From tens of thousands of miles,
Blows the long-travelling wind
    through Yu Men Guan[2].

The Hans descended Bai Deng Road[3];
The Tartars spied on Qing Hai Wan[4].

From battlefields since ancient times,
Returned not a single man.

Warriors gaze at the border town:
Many look miserable,
    yearning to return to their clan.

On this night at home in tall houses,
Their loved ones would sigh and sigh …
    stop they hardly can.

明月出天山，
蒼茫雲海間。

長風幾萬里，
吹度玉門關。

漢下白登道，
胡窺青海灣。

由來征戰地，
不見有人還。

戍客望邊邑，
思歸多苦顏。

高樓當此夜，
嘆息應未閒。

---

1 One of the largest mountains in northwestern China.

2 Border pass in ancient northwest China, also known as Jade Pass or Yu Men Guan in Dunhuang, Gansu Province.

3 The original name of this place is Bai Deng Terrace （白登台）. This is the place where Liu Bang （漢高 祖劉邦）, the Emperor of the West Han Dynasty （西漢漢高祖）(B.C. 206 — B.C. 195) was besieged by the tartars for seven days. It is now in the east of Datong, Shaanxi Province.

4 East of Qinghai Province. The tartars (barbarians who made raids on Chinese towns from time to time in ancient times) were still keeping a stealthy watch in Tang Dynasty.

CROWS CAWING AT NIGHT

Li Bai (701 — 762)

Crows flock to their nests
　　on the city's fringe at twilight:
They chatter on the branches
　　after their homeward flight.

Weaving brocade by the loom
　　is a Qin Chuan[1] dame;
The green gauze looks like mist
　　as she murmurs behind the window pane.

In sadness she stops the shuttle –
　　recalling her love faraway:
Alone lying in bed in an empty room,
　　her tears fall like rain.

烏夜啼

李白 (701 — 762)

黃雲城邊烏欲棲，
歸飛啞啞枝上啼。

機中織錦秦川女，
碧紗如煙隔窗語。

停梭悵然憶遠人，
獨宿空房淚如雨。

1　Name of a place in Shaanxi Province.

Seeing Meng Haoran off at Yellow Crane Tower

Li Bai (701 — 762)

黄鶴樓送孟浩然
之廣陵

李白（701 — 762）

My dear friend, on the west side of
　　Yellow Crane Tower[1] you bid me adieu:
Amid the third month's mist and flowers,
　　downstream to Yangzhou you go.

Into the blue horizon,
　　the distant shadow of a lone sail vanishes;
Towards the sky,
　　only the Yangtze River is seen to flow.

故人西辭黄鶴樓，
煙花三月下揚州。

孤帆遠影碧空盡，
惟見長江天際流。

1　A famous ancient tower on the bank of Yangtze River in
　　Wuhan County, Hubei Province. It was so named after a
　　sage who once stopped by this tower long ago and left on
　　the back of a yellow crane according to the legend. The
　　poet's friend sailed eastward to Yangzhou from this tower.

A GUEST'S SONG

Li Bai (701 — 762)

客中行

李白（701 — 762）

Fine wine of Lanling[1]
    with the fragrance of tulip is brought:
It glitters like amber in a jade pot.

If only the host can make the guest drunk,
Where home is he'd know not[2].

蘭陵美酒鬱金香，
玉碗盛來琥珀光。

但使主人能醉客，
不知何處是他鄉。

1　Name of a place in ancient Shandong Province famous for its fine wine.
2　The poet was staying far away from home and was feeling home-sick.　He would forget he was in other
   people's home when he was drunk.

DIFFICULT IS THE WAY

Li Bai (701 — 762)

Gold jugs of clear wine
    at ten thousand coins a pint;
Jade dishes of delicacies beyond all price.

My cup I lower, chopsticks I drop,
    having lost my appetite;
My sword I draw, looking around –
    my mind blankness occupies.

The Yellow River I wish to cross
    but it's blocked by ice;
The Tai Hang[1] I intend to climb
    but snow darkens the skies.

At my leisure, I go fishing by an emerald stream… .
Suddenly I'm back in my boat dreaming
    of the place beside which the sun lies[2].

Difficult is the way!
Difficult is the way!

Too many crossroads:
Now where can my way be?

Ripe will be the time to ride out
    the turbulent winds and waves,
When I'll hoist the sail straight into the clouds
    and cross the boundless sea.

行路難

李白 (701 — 762)

金樽清酒斗十千，玉盤珍饈值萬錢。
停杯投箸不能食，拔劍四顧心茫然。

欲渡黃河冰塞川，將登太行雪暗天。
閒來垂釣碧溪上，忽復乘舟夢日邊。

行路難！行路難！
多歧路，今安在？

長風破浪會有時，直掛雲帆濟滄海。

1 The Tai Hang Mountain which lies between the Great Wall and the Yellow River in Shanxi Province.
2 According to writings in the East Jin Dynasty (東晉朝 A.D. 317 — A.D. 420), the Jin Emperor (晉明帝 A.D. 323 — A.D. 326) reckoned that the place where he lived (he being the Son of Heaven 天子) was closest to the sun. In ancient China, the sun symbolized the Emperor and that it lay beside the capital. Li Bai dreamed he was in the capital.

Background:
The poet longed for an opportunity to serve his country in the Imperial Court. He was depressed as the road to get an appointment was treacherous. He lost his appetite before fine wine and good food. However, he was still optimistic as can be seen in the last stanza of the poem.

SONG OF SPRING

Li Bai (701 — 762)

春歌

子夜四時歌之一

李白（701 — 762）

A maiden called Luo Fu in Qin;[1]
Picks mulberry leaves
    by the green water on a mound.

Adorning the green branches
    are her fair arms;
Shining in the white sun, her red gown.

"I've to leave to feed the hungry silk-worms:
The five-horse carriage[2]
    shouldn't be hanging around."

秦地羅敷女，
採桑綠水邊。

素手青條上，
紅粧白日鮮。

蠶飢妾欲去，
五馬莫留連。

1   The former domain of the ancient kingdom of Qin (B.C. 221 — B.C. 206). It is now around the
    Shaanxi Province.

2   In ancient times, the chief government official of a district (太守) used to travel in a carriage driven by
    five horses. Here the poet hinted that the official was unwilling to leave the scene.

SONG OF SUMMER

Li Bai (701 — 762)

夏歌

子夜四時歌之二

李白（701 — 762）

The Mirror Lake spans three hundred miles;
Into lotuses, the buds unfold.

Xishi[1] comes in the fifth month:
Around her, admirers swarm –
    too many for Ruo Ye[2] to hold.

"Go back – you needn't work till moonrise:
You'd be called to the Yue[3] Palace," she's told.

鏡湖三百里，
菡萏發荷花。

五月西施來，
人看隘若耶。

回舟不待月，
歸去越王家。

1 A girl in the kingdom of Yue in the East Zhou Dynasty (B.C. 770 — B.C. 256) who was known all over ancient China for her peerless beauty.

2 Name of a stream near the Mirror Lake and flows into it.

3 An ancient kingdom in the East Zhou Dynasty (B.C. 770 — B.C. 256).

Background:
Xi Shi was a clothes-washing girl by the Ruo Ye Stream. She became the beloved concubine of King Yue (越王勾踐 B.C. 496 — B.C. 464) because of her matchless beauty. Yue was later conquered by Wu and she was given to King Wu as part of Yue's plot. Such a move resulted in the downfall of the Kingdom of Wu. King Yue eventually regained his kingdom.

SONG OF AUTUMN

Li Bai (701 — 762)

秋 歌

子夜四時歌之三

李白（701 — 762）

A strip of moon
　　　hangs over Chang'an[1],
Amid ten thousand families'
　　　clothes-pounding[2] sound.

Never can the autumn wind blow it away –
My love for Yu Guan[3] is profound.

When will the Huns[4] be defeated?
My husband would then be homeward-bound.

長安一片月，
萬戶搗衣聲。

秋風吹不盡，
總是玉關情。

何日平胡虜，
良人罷遠征。

1　Capital city in Tang Dynasty. It is now called Xi'an.

2　In ancient times, people washed clothes by pounding them with a wood club in water.

3　Border pass in ancient northwestern China, also known as Jade Pass or Yu Men Guan in Dunhuang County, Gansu Province.

4　Also known as Xiongnu. These were barbarians who made raids on Chinese towns from time to time along the northeast border in ancient times.

SONG OF WINTER

Li Bai (701 — 762)

The courier is due to set off in the morning:
Throughout the night,
  a warrior's cotton robe I sew.

Pulling the needle,
  my bare hands are freezing;
The scissors too cold to hold, oh!

The robe is made for dispatch
  to a faraway place,
When will it reach Lin Tao[1] so?

冬歌

子夜四時歌之四

李白（701 — 762）

明朝驛使發，
一夜絮征袍。

素手抽鍼冷，
那堪把剪刀。

裁縫寄遠道，
幾日到臨洮。

1　Min County (岷縣) in present day Gansu Province bordering Tibet. It was the starting point of the ancient Great Wall.

GAZING AT HEAVEN GATE MOUNT[1]

Li Bai (701 — 762)

望天門山

李白 (701 — 762)

On rushes the Chu river[2] –
    splitting of Heaven Gate Mount is done;
Around it, swirls the emerald water
    on its eastward run.

Green mountains stretch out from the shores;
A lone sail comes from the direction of the sun.

天門中斷楚江開，
碧水東流至此回。

兩岸青山相對出，
孤帆一片日邊來。

---

1 A name referring to two mountains, the East Liang Mountain and the West Liang Mountain in Anhui Province. These two mountains when seen together in the distance resemble a huge gate broken open by the Chu River running in between.

2 Name of a section of the Yangtze River so called because it runs through the former domain of the ancient Kingdom of Chu (楚國) in the Zhou Dynasty (B.C. 1046 — B.C. 256). It is located in today's Anhui Province.

PLAINT

Li Bai (701 — 762)

A lady rolls up the beaded curtain;
She sits with a frown till late.

Seen only are wet tear stains;
Known not whom she may hate.

怨情

李白（701 — 762）

美人捲珠簾，
深坐顰娥眉。

但見淚痕濕，
不知心恨誰。

PURE SERENE MUSIC (1)

Li Bai (701 — 762)

清平調 （I）

李白 (701 — 762)

From the clouds you think of her dresses,
　　from the flowers her face;
A spring breeze caresses the rail,
　　pearls of dew roll with grace.

If not seen atop the Jade Mountain[1],
You would meet her
　　under the moon in the Jade Terrace[2].

雲想衣裳花想容，
春風拂檻露華濃。

若非群玉山頭見，
會向瑤臺月下逢。

Background:
This and the other two poems following were specially written by Li Bai to praise Yang Gui Fei (楊貴妃) while he was serving as a poet in the Tang Palace. He was summoned to the palace garden during an occasion when Emperor Tang Xuan Zong (唐玄宗) was admiring peony with Yang Gui Fei (楊貴妃), his beloved and controversial concubine.

Note:
1 Residence of the Goddess of the West (西王母) according to the legend.
2 Residence of fairies according to the legend. It was made of precious jade.

PURE SERENE MUSIC (2)

Li Bai (701 — 762)

清平調 （2）

李白（701 — 762）

Like a dewy scarlet peony, she[1] is so sweet,
But the Goddess of Wushan[2]
　　is heartbreaking to meet.

With her who in the Han Palace
　　can compare?
Even the lovely Fei Yan[3] relied on
　　new make-ups to look a treat.

一枝紅艷露凝香，
雲雨巫山枉斷腸。

借問漢宮誰得似，
可憐飛燕倚新妝。

1　Yang Gui Fei (楊貴妃). Li Bai compared her with a scarlet peony, the prettiest and noblest of all flowers in China.

2　Ancient legend has it that Emperor Chor (楚王) once had a secret meeting with the Goddess of Wu Shan (巫山 i.e. the mountain in the Three Gorges near Chonqing) in his dream on a rainy night during his hunting trip in Wu Shan. When the Emperor woke up the next morning, the Goddess could not be found. Only a sharp peak surrounded by clouds was seen. The Emperor was heartbroken. This sharp peak was later called the Goddess Peak (神女峯). It was also known that the Goddess would appear in the form of clouds in the morning and rain at night (旦為朝雲，暮為行雨) and could be met only in a dream.

3　Fei Yan (i.e. Zhao Fei Yan) was a great beauty in the Han Dynasty in the 1st century B.C.. She was the beloved queen of Han Emperor Chengdi. The legend says she was a great dancer. She was so slim and delicate that she could dance on a man's palm. Here the poet questioned she relied on make-ups to keep her beauty. In contrast, the poet hinted Yang Gui Fei was a 100% natural beauty and was beyond compare.

PURE SERENE MUSIC (3)

Li Bai (701 — 762)

清平調　（３）

李白（701 — 762）

A rare flower, a stunning beauty,
    the Emperor's favour she's set to win.
Often she attracts
    his gaze with a grin.

The deep regrets of spring[1]
    annoying him she dispels —
Leaning against the balustrade,
    north of the scented pavilion they're in.

名花傾國兩相歡，
常得君王帶笑看。

解釋春風無限恨，
沉香亭北倚欄杆。

---

1 In the spring of the 25th year of Kai Yuan (開元), Wu Hui Fei (武惠妃), the Tang Emperor's beloved concubine died. The Emperor had since been unhappy and regretful until he met Yang Gui Fei.

FAREWELL TO A FRIEND

Li Bai (701 — 762)

Beyond the northern walls,
    blue mountains rise;
Around the eastern city, white waters flow.

Farewell I bid you here;
Away ten thousand miles you drift,
    like lone tumbleweeds in the wind blow.

The floating clouds convey
    a traveller's sentiment;
The setting sun the affection to a friend I owe.

Upon waving of hands and
    the neigh of horses,
Alone, off you go.

送友人

李白（701 — 762）

青山橫北郭，
白水繞東城。

此地一為別，
孤蓬萬里征。

浮雲遊子意，
落日故人情。

揮手自茲去，
蕭蕭班馬鳴。

TO MENG HAORAN

Li Bai (701 — 762)

贈孟浩然

李白 (701 — 762)

I adore you, Master Meng!
Beneath the heaven,
　　　your great talents are known best.

Ruddy-cheeked, you renounced carriage and cap[1];
Whitehaired,
　　　among pines under white clouds you rest[2].

An habitual drinker under the moon,
Unwilling to serve the Emperor
　　　but by flowers you're obsessed.

Like a towering mountain,
　　　you're beyond reach:
My salute to you,
　　　a man of virtue the highest!

吾愛孟夫子，
風流天下聞。

紅顏棄軒冕，
白首臥松雲。

醉月頻中聖，
迷花不事君。

高山安可仰，
徒此揖清芬。

1　A person appointed by the Court would be granted official carriage for his own use and a special cap to wear when attending Court sessions.

2　Living in the country close to nature among pine trees under white clouds was regarded as good virtue among scholars in the old days.

QUESTION AND ANSWER
IN THE MOUNTAIN

Li Bai (701 — 762)

I stay in this emerald mountain and
  you ask, "What are the reasons behind?"
I smile but answer not
  for I've a carefree mind.

Peach blossoms flow with running water
  into the unknown:
I'm in another world,
  not the world of mankind.

山中問答

李白 (701 — 762)

問余何事棲碧山，
笑而不答心自閒。

桃花流水杳然去，
別有天地非人間。

TO WANG LUN

Li Bai (701 — 762)

Li Bai was about to set sail in a sampan,
When suddenly
  someone on the shore stamped and sang.

Water in the Peach Blossom Pool
  is a thousand feet deep,
But not so deep as the affection of Wang.

贈汪倫

李白 (701 — 762)

李白乘舟將欲行，
忽聞岸上踏歌聲。

桃花潭水深千尺，
不及汪倫送我情。

AT A FAREWELL BANQUET FOR SHU YUN, THE OFFICIAL EDITOR, IN XIE TIAO TOWER, XUANZHOU

Li Bai (701 — 762)

That which abandoned me –
  yesterday was a day couldn't be made to stay;
That which disturbs my heart –
  today is a day of troubles and dismay.

Through ten thousand miles,
  the wind carries the autumn wild geese:
Facing this scene on the tower,
  drink our fill we may!

Your writings are of
  Jian-an style[1] typical of Penglai[2],
Inside which Xie's[3] purity and freshness lie.

They exhilarate and stimulate the desire to fly –
Wishing to clasp the moon in the blue sky!

Draw a knife and cut the water –
  the water would nevertheless flow;
Raise a cup to dispel your woe –
  woe comes after woe.

My life in this world
  matches not my aspirations:
Tomorrow morning,
  with loosened hair, a little boat I'll row.

宣州謝朓樓餞別校書叔雲

李白（701 — 762）

棄我去者，昨日之日不可留。
亂我心者，今日之日多煩憂。
長風萬里送秋雁，對此可以酣高樓。

蓬萊文章建安骨，中間小謝又清發。
俱懷逸興壯思飛，欲上青天攬明月。

抽刀斷水水更流，舉杯消愁愁更愁。
人生在世不稱意，明朝散髮弄扁舟。

1 A school of writing first gained recognition in the Han Dynasty (B.C. 206 — A.D. 220) and later became well-known in Wei Dynasty (A.D. 220 — A.D. 265) of the Three Kingdoms Period for being full of passion and stimulating.

2 The nick name of Xuanzhou in which Shu Yun served as the Official Editor.

3 Xie Tiao, the former head of the capital of Xuanzhou and a celebrated scholar after whom the tower was named.

Background:

While writing a farewell poem for his friend, Li Bai took the opportunity to air his grievance of not being able to use his talents for the good of his country as clearly reflected in the last four lines of this poem.

JADE STEPS PLAINT

Li Bai (701 — 762)

White grows the dew on the jade steps –
Wetting her silk stockings in the long night.

She then lowers the crystal curtain,
Gazing at the autumn moon, clear and bright.

玉階怨

李白 （701 — 762）

玉階生白露，
夜久侵羅襪。

卻下水晶簾，
玲瓏望秋月。

FAREWELL AT JING MEN[1]

Li Bai (701 — 762)

Sailing far beyond Jing Men,
On a tour to the state of Chu we go.

Into the open country,
　　mountains wind down;
Onto vast moorland, rivers flow.

The moon descends
　　like a mirror[2] from the sky;
The clouds rise and a mirage is on show.

We should love the water of our homeland:

To bid you farewell,
　　a ten-thousand-mile journey it'd undergo.

渡荊門送別

李白（701 — 762）

渡遠荊門外，
來從楚國遊。

山隨平野盡，
江入大荒流。

月下飛天鏡，
雲生結海樓。

仍憐故鄉水，
萬里送行舟。

---

1 A place to the east of the former state of Chu in the Warring Period (B.C. 475 — B.C. 221). It was in today's Hubei Province. Li Bai accompanied his departing friend until after they had passed Jing Men.

2 The moon was reflected in the river.

YELLOW CRANE TOWER[1]

Cui Hao (around 704? — 754)

Gone was the sage riding a yellow crane:
The Yellow Crane Tower is all that remained.

Never did the yellow crane return:
For a thousand years, white clouds waited in vain.

So vivid are the Yangtze[2] and
   the trees of Hanyang[3] in the sun;
So lush the sweet grass on the Parrots Domain[4].

Where's my hometown, now dusk is near?
On this misty river, sorrows reign.

---

1 A famous ancient tower first built in A.D. 223 on the bank of Yangtze River in Wuhan county, Hubei Province. It was named as such after the depature of a sage from the tower long ago on the back of a yellow crane according the legend.

2 The Yangtze River.

3 Hanyang county, Hubei Province.

4 An isle inhabited by parrots in the Yangtze River southwest of Hanyang County.

黃鶴樓

崔顥（大約 704? － 754 年）

昔人已乘黃鶴去，
此地空餘黃鶴樓。

黃鶴一去不復返，
白雲千載空悠悠。

晴川歷歷漢陽樹，
芳草萋萋鸚鵡洲。

日暮鄉關何處是，
煙波江上使人愁。

THE SONG OF CHANG GAN[1] (1)

Cui Hao (around 704? — 754)

長干曲 (1)

崔顥 （大約 704? — 754 年）

Where do you live, sir?
I live in Heng Tang[2].

I stop my boat briefly to ask –
Just in case we belong to the same clan.

君家何處住，
妾住在橫塘。

停船暫借問，
或恐是同鄉。

---

1 Name of a place in today's Nanjing.
2 Today's Jin Ling County in Jiangsu Province.

THE SONG OF CHANG GAN (2)

Cui Hao (around 704? — 754)

長干曲 (2)

崔顥〔大約 704? — 754 年〕

My home lies beside a river in Jiujiang[1]:
Along the river I travel to and fro.

We're both natives of Chang Gan[2]:
We were small then – each other we didn't know.

家臨九江水，
來去九江側。

同是長干人，
生小不相識。

---

1 Jiujiang County along the Yangtze River in Jiangxi Province.
2 Name of a place in today's Nanjing.

Looking In Vain for a Recluse

Jia Dao (793 — 865)

尋隱者不遇

賈島（793 — 865）

A boy I asked beneath a pine tree.
"My master went gathering herbs", replied he.

"Somewhere in this mountain,
Deep behind the clouds but
  his whereabouts not known to me".

松下問童子，
言師採藥去。

只在此山中，
雲深不知處。

A GIRL OF A POOR FAMILY

Qin Taoyu (year of birth and death unknown)

貧女

秦韜玉 （生卒年不詳）

A girl under a thatched roof [1] knows not
    what fine silk and perfume can do;
A matchmaker she wishes to employ but
    is sad her humble origin interests few.

Who'd admire
    a pristine character with good taste?
Deplorable is the trend of
    showy make-up on view.

She refuses to compete
    in extending eyebrows,
But at delicate needlework, she excels in lieu.

How resentful to embroider
    in gold threads year after year,
Only to make bridal gowns
    for other couples new.

蓬門未識綺羅香，
擬託良媒亦自傷。

誰愛風流高格調，
共憐時世儉梳妝。

敢將十指誇針巧，
不把雙眉鬥畫長。

苦恨年年壓金線，
為他人作嫁衣裳。

---

1 This means the home of a poor family. In old China, rich families lived in houses with tiled roofs.

PROSPECT OF SPRING

Du Fu (712 — 770)

春望

杜甫（712 — 770）

The Empire has crumbled —
    only mountains and rivers remain;
Grass and trees grow thick,
    as the city awakes in spring.

Grieving the situation,
    flowers splash their tears;
Lamenting the separation,
    birds startle me as they sing.

Nonstop for three months,
    beacon fires flare:
A home letter's worth only
    ten thousand pieces of gold can bring.

Scratching my white head shortens the hair:
Indeed too short for a hairpin to cling.

國破山河在，
城春草木深。

感時花濺淚，
恨別鳥驚心。

烽火連三月，
家書抵萬金。

白頭搔更短，
渾欲不勝簪。

Background:
This poem was written in A.D. 757 after the capital Chang'an (長安) fell into the hands of the rebellion army during the An Lushan Rebellion (安史之亂 A.D. 755 — A.D. 763). The Tang Emperor Xuanzong (唐玄宗) escaped to Sichuan. Du Fu was stranded in Chang'an. He was saddened by the deplorable situation of his country and the separation from his family by non-stop fighting.

THE PRIME MINISTER OF SHU[1]

Du Fu (712 — 770)

Where can we find the shrine of the Master[2]?
Outside the Brocade Officers City[3]
      where cypresses grow in a thick cluster.

Gleaming on the steps, the emerald grass
      displays the colours of spring unnoticed;
Behind the leaves, the sweet songs
      of orioles add not to the lustre.

Great were the Three Visits[4]
      and the scheme for an Empire!
Great were you in founding and stabilizing
      the two Reigns on supports you mustered!

How sad you died before the battle was won:
Heroes shed tears on their armours ever after!

1 The Kingdom of Shu (蜀國) in the Three Kingdoms Period (A.D. 220 — A.D. 280).

2 Zhuge Liang (諸葛亮即孔明), well-known as the Master of Tactics. He was the prime minister of the Kingdom of Shu (蜀國) in the Three Kingdoms Period with Chengdu as its capital.

3 Today's City of Chengdu (成都), the capital city of of the Sichuan Province.

4 Liu Bei (劉備), the first ruler of the Kingdom of Shu paid three humble visits to Zhuge Liang's cottage and convinced him to come out to assist him in his fighting campaigns and in founding and strengthening his empire. After Liu Bei's death, Zhuge Liang continued to assist his heir, Liu Shan, in his reign. Zhuge Liang died in A.D. 234 during an expedition against the State of Wei before the battle was won.

蜀相

杜甫（712 — 770）

丞相祠堂何處尋，
錦官城外柏森森。

映階碧草自春色，
隔葉黃鸝空好音。

三顧頻煩天下計，
兩朝開濟老臣心。

出師未捷身先死，
長使英雄淚滿襟。

THOUGHTS ON A NIGHT JOURNEY

Du Fu (712 — 770)

Amid slender grass and
      light breeze by the shore,
At night, is moored a tall-mast solitary sampan.

Above the big rolling river, the moon surges;
Over the boundless wild, the stars hang.

One shouldn't come to fame
      by virtue of his writings:
Old and sick, my retirement I should plan.

Drifting endlessly, what do I resemble?
A lone gull in between the sky and the land.

Background:
This poem was written in A.D. 765 when Du Fu was on his way to take up a new post in Yuan Yang County in Sichuan. The poet felt a bit downcast to be drifting around to take up new posts even at the age of 53. It can be seen that people considered themselves old when they reached the age of 50 in ancient times.

旅夜書懷

杜甫（712 — 770）

細草微風岸，
危檣獨夜舟。

星垂平野闊，
月湧大江流。

名豈文章著，
官應老病休。

飄飄何所似，
天地一沙鷗。

ARRIVAL OF A GUEST

(Rejoicing at the arrival of Magistrate Cui)

Du Fu (712 — 770)

North and south of my cottage,
    runs the spring flood tide;
Day after day, only gulls
    are seen in flocks coming by.

Never has the flowery path
    been swept for a guest;
For you today for the first time,
    the wicker gate open I.

Far from the market,
    few dishes can I serve;
In a poor family,
    only stale wine can I supply.

Would you like drinking together
    with my elder neighbour?
Across the fence him I'll call
    to drink our last cups dry.

客至

（崔縣令到訪喜不自勝）

杜甫（712 — 770）

舍南舍北皆春水，
但見群鷗日日來。

花徑不曾緣客掃，
蓬門今始為君開。

盤飧市遠無兼味，
樽酒家貧只舊醅。

肯與鄰翁相對飲？
隔籬呼取盡餘杯。

A POEM FOR HUA-QING [1]

Du Fu (712 — 770)

Day after day lutes and flutes
    run riot in the City of Brocade [2];
Half of the music goes with the river breeze,
    half into the clouds would fade.

Such tunes should only belong to Heaven:
On earth, how rarely can we hear them played?

贈花卿

杜甫 (712 — 770)

錦城絲管日紛紛，
半入江風半入雲。

此曲只應天上有，
人間能得幾回聞。

---

1 A friend of the poet and a high-ranking official in the city. The poet hinted that he did not observe the rules in playing music which was exclusively reserved for the Emperor in the Court — i.e. music which belongs to Heaven. Emperors in ancient times were regarded as sons of Heaven.

2 Nickname of Chengdu (成都), the capital city of Sichuan Province which was famous for its brocade (decorative cloth with a raised pattern of gold or silk thread).

THOUGHTS ON MY VISIT TO A HISTORIC SITE

Du Fu (712 — 770)

詠懷古跡

杜甫（712 — 770）

Through myriad hills and vales,
    we've come to Jing Men[1]
Where Zhaojun's[2] native village
    still stands as a historic site.

Gone was she from the Imperial Palace
    to the northern desert:
Only a green tomb is left to face the twilight.

Her pretty face is seen only in paintings;
Her soul returns in vain with the
    tingling of girdle-gems in a moonlit night.

For a thousand years, her pi-pa
    accompanies barbarian songs:
Its tunes certainly reveal her rueful plight.

群山萬壑赴荊門，
生長明妃尚有村。

一去紫臺連朔漠，
獨留青塚對黃昏。

圖畫省識春風面，
環珮空歸月夜魂。

千載琵琶作胡語，
分明怨恨此中論。

---

1 A place in the south of Jing Men County in Hubei Province.

2 Wang Zhao Jun（王昭君）, a beauty at the Imperial Court in the Han Dynasty (B.C. 206 — A.D. 220). She was given to a Tartar Chief in B.C. 33 as a gift to appease the Tartars. She spent her lonesome life in the desert accompanied only by her beloved pipa (similar to a lute).

CLIMBING A HEIGHT

Du Fu (712 — 770)

Sharp is the wind under a high sky
    amid the gibbons' howls of woe;
Pure is the islet and its white sand
    with birds flying above to and fro.

Boundless is the forest
    where leaves rustle and fall;
Endless is the Yangtze[1] that comes
    rolling down with its powerful flow.

Ten thousand miles from home and
    saddened in autumn, often I travel;
One hundred years plagued with sickness,
    alone up the terrace I go.

Hardships, sufferings and regrets
    have added frost to my temples;
Disappointed and unsuccessful in life,
    lately drinking I've to forgo[2].

登高

杜甫〔712 — 770〕

風急天高猿嘯哀，
渚清沙白鳥飛迴。

無邊落木蕭蕭下，
不盡長江滾滾來。

萬里悲秋常作客，
百年多病獨登臺。

艱難苦恨繁霜鬢，
潦倒新停濁酒杯。

1　The Yangtze River.
2　The poet had lately stopped drinking because of sickness.

BALLAD OF THE ARMY WAGONS

Du Fu (712 — 770)

Wagons rumble; horses utter long, loud cries;
Soldiers carry bows and arrows on their sides.

Fathers, mothers, wives and children rush to see them off;
Rising dust hides Xianyang Bridge[1] from the eyes.

Pulling the soldiers' clothes and stamping,
    they block the way in tears:
Their wailing shoots into and rends the skies.

A passer-by asks a soldier whose reply is plain,
"Conscription comes again and again."

"At fifteen some were posted north to guard the River[2],
By forty to till the land west we went.

When we left home, village seniors bound our heads[3];
When we returned white-haired – to the border we'd be sent.

At the border, a sea of blood would flow[4],
Yet his grip on border territories
    the Wu[5] Emperor won't let go.

Haven't you heard,
In the two hundred counties east of Hua Mount,
How thorns and thistles in thousands of villages overgrow?

Even where strong women can plough and hoe,
Crops in the fields in utter disorder grow.

Worse still, the hard-fighting Qin[6] soldiers
    Are driven like dogs and chickens to and fro."

兵車行

杜甫 (712 — 770)

車轔轔，馬蕭蕭，行人弓箭各在腰。
爹娘妻子走相送，塵埃不見咸陽橋。
牽衣頓足攔道哭，哭聲直上干雲霄。

道旁過者問行人，行人但云點行頻。

或從十五北防河，便至四十西營田。
去時里正與裹頭，歸來頭白還戍邊。

邊庭流血成海水，武皇開邊意未已。

君不聞，
漢家山東二百州，千村萬落生荊杞？
縱有健婦把鋤犁，禾生隴畝無東西。
況復秦兵耐苦戰，被驅不異犬與雞。

BALLAD OF THE ARMY WAGONS (cont'd)

Du Fu (712 — 770)

"Even though sir, more you want to know,
As conscripts, resentment dare we show?

Just look at the West Pass this winter:
Relief for the soldiers wasn't given consent.

For rent the county officials press hard:
But with what do we pay the tax and rent?

We well know having boys is bad,
But having girls is good.

Boys are doomed to lie buried under wild grasses,
But girls can get married in the neighbourhood."

Don't you see,
By the shores of Qing Hai[7],
The uncollected white bones from of old still lie?

New ghosts grumble, old ghosts sob:
On gloomy, rainy days
one would hear them bitterly cry.

---

1 A large bridge spanning across the Wei River (渭水) in Chang'an (now called Xi'an).

2 In A.D. 728, the upper reaches of the Yellow River were raided by the Tibetan tribesmen. Over 100,000 soldiers were sent to guard the River.

3 The conscripts were so young that they needed village seniors to bind their heads with head cloths before starting a long journey.

4 In the year A.D. 750, tens of thousands of Tang and Tibetan soldiers were killed in border posts in the Stone Fortress (石堡城) campaign.

5 The poet used the word "Wu" (meaning Emperor Wu (漢武帝) (of the Han Dynasty (B.C. 206 — A.D. 220)) instead of "Tang" to avoid punishment. He in fact referred to the Tang Emperor Xuanzong (唐玄宗即唐明皇) who ruled from A.D. 712 to A.D. 756.

6 Ancient name of a region south of the Yellow River.

7 Qing Hai Lake. A large salt water lake by the Yellow River northeast of today's Qinghai Province.

兵車行（續）

杜甫（712 — 770）

長者雖有問，役夫敢申恨？

且如今年冬，未休關西卒。
縣官急索租，租稅從何出？

信知生男惡，反是生女好。
生女猶得嫁比鄰，生男埋沒隨百草。

君不見，
青海頭，古來白骨無人收。
新鬼煩冤舊鬼哭，天陰雨濕聲啾啾。

Background:
The Tang Emperor Xuanzong (唐玄宗) launched many military expeditions beyond the northwest border during his reign. Du Fu was in the capital, Chang'an (長安) in A.D. 752. He was saddened to learn of the Emperor's decadent life style and expansionist mindset. In this poem, Du Fu described the sufferings of the people brought about by non-stop fighting along the border and repeated conscriptions year after year.

GAZING AT TAISHAN[1]

Du Fu (712 — 770)

望嶽

杜甫（712 — 770）

Oh what's Taishan[1] really like?
Its verdure spreads endlessly
　　　from where Qi and Lu[2] meet.

岱宗夫如何？
齊魯青未了。

Nature created this divine grandeur:
Between its north and south[3],
　　　darkness and light are divided neat.

造化鍾神秀，
陰陽割昏曉。

To the rising clouds in tiers, I thrill;
With wide-open eyes, returning birds I greet.

盪胸生層雲，
決眥入歸鳥。

One day I'll make it to the summit:
All mountains will look small under my feet.

會當凌絕頂，
一覽眾山小。

1　A much-revered large mountain located in Shandong Province.

2　These were the two ancient kingdoms in the Warring States Period (B.C. 475 — B.C. 221) that used to lie respectively on the north and south of Taishan.

3　Yin and Yang (陰陽) referred to north and south in this context.

A MOONLIT NIGHT

Du Fu (712 — 770)

月夜

杜甫 (712 — 770)

The moon is over Fuzhou[1] tonight.
In her chamber she alone watches it shine.

Oh! How I miss my little children from afar:
They know not Chang'an[2] to pine.

Her cloud-like hair
    in the sweet mist is damp;
Her jade-like arms
    in the moonlight cold as brine.

When shall we together
    lean against the gauze curtain,
And let the moonlight dry
    the tear-stains, yours and mine?

今夜鄜州月，
閨中只獨看。

遙憐小兒女，
未解憶長安。

香霧雲鬟濕，
清輝玉臂寒。

何時倚虛幌，
雙照淚痕乾。

---

1 Old name of a county in Shaanxi Province. It is now called the Fu County.

2 The capital in Tang Dynasty. Now the city of Xi'an. Du Fu was stranded in Chang'an during the rebellion of An Lu Shan (安祿山) while his family was at home in Fuzhou.

MEETING LI GUINIAN[1]
IN RIVER SOUTH

Du Fu (712 — 770)

江南逢李龜年

杜甫（712 — 770）

Often I saw you in Prince Qi's mansion;
Several times
  I heard you sing in Cui Jiu's[2] hall.

At a time when
  River South boasts fine scenery,
Again I meet you
  in a season when flowers fall.

岐王宅裏尋常見，
崔九堂前幾度聞。

正是江南好風景，
落花時節又逢君。

1　A famous court singer at the time.
2　A high-ranking court official.

REMEMBERING MY BROTHERS IN A MOONLIT NIGHT

Du Fu (712 — 770)

Battle drums halt passers-by;
A wild goose in the autumn frontier utters a cry.

Dewdrops turn white from tonight;
The moon's brighter in my homeland's sky.

My younger brothers are all scattered:
Nowhere can I ask if they still live or have died.

My letters never reach them.
Besides, the end of the battle isn't nigh.

月夜憶舍弟

杜甫 (712 — 770)

戍鼓斷人行，
秋邊一雁聲。

露從今夜白，
月是故鄉明。

有弟皆分散，
無家問死生。

寄書長不達，
況乃未休兵。

Background:
This poem was written in A.D. 759 in Qinzhou (秦州) in an autumn moonlit night. Du Fu fled his home after the capital Chang'an fell into the hands of the rebellion army during the An Lu Shan Rebellion (安史 之亂 A.D. 755 — A.D. 763). He lost contact with his brothers and feared for their lives because fighting had not stopped.

DREAMING OF LI BAI

Du Fu (712 — 770)

Floating clouds sail by all day –
But the traveller hasn't returned yet[1].

You I dreamed of three nights in a row:
Your deep affection for me the dreams reflect.

Often you were in a hurry to leave –
Saying bitterly that coming was quite a sweat.

Rivers and lakes were turbulent:
About mishaps in sailing you'd fret.

You scratched your white head
        while stepping out of the door,
As if your life's ambition had been upset.

Princes and dignitaries pack the capital;
But how miserable you alone get!

Who says 'Heaven's Net spreads far and wide'[2]?
How come at old age[3],
        with misfortunes you're beset?

Your name will be remembered
        through the centuries,
But how lonely after one's fate is met! [4]

夢李白

杜甫（712 — 770）

浮雲終日行，
遊子久不至。

三夜頻夢君，
情親見君意。

告歸常侷促，
苦道來不易。

江湖多風波，
舟楫恐失墜。

出門搔白首，
若負平生志。

冠蓋滿京華，
斯人獨憔悴。

孰云網恢恢，
將老身反累。

千秋萬歲名，
寂寞身後事。

---

1 Li Bai was banished to a remote place called Ye Lang (夜郎) in today's Guizhou Province (貴州) in ancient southwest China in A.D. 755 for his connection with a fight for the throne by Li Lin (李璘), the brother of the Tang Emperor, Li Xiang (李亨即肅宗 A.D. 756 — A.D. 762). The poet heard no news of him for a long time.

2 A quotation from the *Dao De Jing* (《道德經》) meaning that everything on earth is kept inside a huge invisible net being closely watched by Heaven. Injustice will not be unchecked and wrongs will be righted in due course.

3 Li Bai was 59 years old when he was banished.

4 The poet feared Li Bai could have died on his long and treacherous way to take up his new post.

THINKING OF LI BAI AT SKY'S END

Du Fu (712 — 770)

天末懷李白

杜甫（712 — 770）

Cold is the wind that rises
　　　at the sky's end:
My dear friend, how do you feel inside?

When will your letters arrive?
Rivers and lakes are swollen
　　　with the autumn flood tide.

Good writing is at odds with prosperity;
People's faults evil spirits love to deride.

Drop your poems into the Mi Luo River[1]:
To the resentful ghost[2],

　　　all the misfortunes you should confide.

涼風起天末，
君子意如何？

鴻雁幾時到，
江湖秋水多。

文章憎命達，
魑魅喜人過。

應共冤魂語，
投詩贈汨羅。

1　A river in Hunan Province in which Qu Yuan (屈原) drowned himself while living in exile in despair.

2　The spirit of Qu Yuan (屈原), a great patriotic poet of the Kingdom of Chu (楚國) in the Warring States Period (B.C. 475 — B.C. 221).

Background:
This poem was written in A.D. 759. At the time Li Bai was in exile in a small remote protectorate in the southwest called Ye Lang (夜郎) (in today's Guizhou Province (貴州)). It was believed this place was full of evil mountain and river spirits. Many however thought Du Fu actually meant Li Bai's exile was the result of vilification by evil officials in the court who were jealous of his talents.

THE "EIGHT BATTLE FORMATION PLANS" [1]

Du Fu (712 — 770)

His exploits eclipsed all
　　in the Three Kingdoms[2];
His "Eight Battle Formation Plans"
　　brought him fame.

On flows the river but the stones[3] roll not:
Shu[4] failed to conquer Wu – what a shame!

八陣圖

杜甫（712 — 770）

功蓋三分國，
名成八陣圖。

江流石不轉，
遺恨失吞吳。

1　Strategic plans for formation of troops in battles devised by Zhuge Liang (諸葛亮即孔明), a minister of the Kingdom of Shu (蜀國). The Plans brought many victories to the Shu army against their enemies.

2　Zhuge Liang's wisdom surpassed all in the Three Kingdoms Period (A.D. 220 — A.D. 280).

3　Stones which were used by Zhuge Liang to mark his formation plans still stayed in their location.

4　Liu Bei (劉備), the King of Shu (蜀國), launched an attack on Wu (吳國) against the advice of Zhuge Liang. He lost the battle and was killed.

TO MR WEI, THE EIGHTH

Du Fu (712 — 770)

In life, friends rarely meet:
Like morning and evening stars,
    each goes its own way.

What a night indeed is tonight!
The same candlelight share we may.

How long can we stay young and strong?
Our temples have all turned grey.

Half of our friends we visited
    have become ghosts –
We cry out in shock and dismay.

Who knows after twenty years,
Again to your home I've taken my way?

You were unmarried when we last parted;
Suddenly your children line up in proud array.

Happily paying respect to their father's friend,
From where I came ask they.

Before the dialogue ends,
With wine and dishes,
    the table your children lay.

Spring leeks gathered in the night rain;
Rice and millet freshly cooked in a medley.

You say it's hard for us to meet:
Ten cups we each empty right away.

We aren't drunk after ten cups –
I'm moved by the deep affection you display.

Tomorrow we'll be separated by mountains... .
How worldly affairs would unfold isn't for us to say.

贈衛八處士

杜甫 (712 — 770)

人生不相見，動如參與商。
今夕復何夕，共此燈燭光。

少壯能幾時，鬢髮各已蒼。
訪舊半為鬼，驚呼熱中腸。

焉知二十載，重上君子堂。
昔別君未婚，兒女忽成行。

怡然敬父執，問我來何方。
問答未及已，兒女羅酒漿。

夜雨剪春韭，新炊間黃粱。
主稱會面難，一舉累十觴。

十觴亦不醉，感君故意長。
明日隔山嶽，世事兩茫茫。

Background:
In this poem the poet showed his affection to an old friend he visited after they parted for 20 years. He also recorded his feelings about the ups and downs in life that nobody could foresee but all had to face, especially in the last two lines of the poem.

LOOKING OUT IN THE COUNTRYSIDE

Du Fu (712 — 770)

野望

杜甫（712 — 770）

Under the snowy West Mount[1],
    the three towns[2] are heavily guarded;
Across the Clear River from the south shore,
    the Myriad Mile Bridge is seen to extend.

Separated from my younger brothers
    by turmoil all over the country,
I'm shedding tears from afar at the world's end.

Not the slightest have I contributed
    to the Imperial Court:
Aging, my declining years
    much sickness would attend.

At times I ride to the countryside
    for a distant view:
How unbearable,
    the situation's on a downward trend.

西山白雪三城戍，
南浦清江萬里橋。

海內風塵諸弟隔，
天涯涕淚一身遙。

唯將遲暮供多病，
未有涓滴答聖朝。

跨馬出郊時極目，
不堪人事日蕭條。

---

1 A snowy mountain in the west of Chengdu in Sichuan Province.

2 These are Songzhou, Weizhou and Paozhou on the frontier bordering Turfan land.

Background:
This poem was written in A.D. 761 during the An Lu Shan Rebellion (安史之亂 A.D. 755 — A.D. 763).
Increasing warfare was waged everywhere. Du Fu was separated from his family and he felt the situation
was unbearable.

FIGHTING AT THE BORDER

Du Fu (712 — 770)

When drawing a bow,
　　one's pull must be strong;
The arrow one uses must be long.

Shoot the horse before shooting the rider;
Capture the leader
　　before capturing the looting throng.

Killing would be limited and
States can keep peace their borders along.

If invasions and humiliations can be quelled,
What's the need for killings to go on?

前出塞

杜甫 (712 — 770)

挽弓當挽強，
用箭當用長。

射人先射馬，
擒賊先擒王。

殺人亦有限，
列國自有疆。

苟能制侵凌，
豈在多殺傷。

UNTITLED (1)

Du Fu (712 — 770)

Atop an emerald willow,
    two golden orioles twitter;
Toward the blue sky,
    a row of egrets float.

Through the window is seen
    the Western Range's everlasting snow;
By the gate is moored
    East Wu's[1] myriad-mile boat.

絕句 （Ⅰ）

杜甫（712 — 770）

兩個黃鸝鳴翠柳，
一行白鷺上青天。

窗含西嶺千秋雪，
門泊東吳萬里船。

---

1 The Kingdom of East Wu was many thousands miles north of the Yangtze River.

UNTITLED (2)

Du Fu (712 — 770)

So blue is the river
    that birds look dazzling white;
So green is the hill
    that flowers seem to burn.

This spring will soon pass,
But when can I return?

絕句 （2）

杜甫 （712 — 770）

江碧鳥逾白，
山青花欲燃。

今春看又過，
何日是歸年。

MY ANSWER TO SOMEONE

A Recluse (7ᵗʰ Century)

答人

太上隱者（七世紀）

"I chanced to come under a pine tree:
On a rock I slept carefree[1].

No calendar is there in the mountain:
The cold spell has ended
　　　but the year[2] is not known to me."

偶來松樹下，
高枕石頭眠。

山中無曆日，
寒盡不知年。

1　The words "高枕" referred to a Chinese saying "高枕無憂" meaning 'sleeping carefree'.

2　The recluse said he had no idea of what year it was as there was no calendar in the mountain.

AN OLD FISHERMAN

Liu Zongyuan (773 — 819)

An old fisherman spent the night
　　the Western Cliff[1] below.
Clear water he drew from the Xiang River,
　　bamboo of Chu[2] he burnt at cockcrow.

Not a soul he sees at sunrise
　　as the smoke disperses;
Green turn the mountains and water
　　at the creak of oars as he starts to row.

Looking back,
　　the sky's afloat in the water;
Above the cliff,
　　mindless clouds chase each other to and fro.

漁翁

柳宗元〔773 — 819〕

漁翁夜傍西巖宿，
曉汲清湘燃楚竹。

煙銷日出不見人，
欸乃一聲山水綠。

回看天際下中流，
巖上無心雲相逐。

1　The Western Mountain in Hunan Province.
2　A type of bamboo commonly found in the former Kingdom of Chu in southern China.

CLIMBING THE LIUZHOU CITY TOWER, A POEM SENT TO THE PREFECTS OF ZHANGZHOU, DINGZHOU, FENGZHOU AND LIANZHOU

Liu Zhongyuan (773 — 819)

The tower on the city wall
    adjoins the vast wilderness;
Endless are the sea and sky…
    and the melancholy thoughts in my mind.

The scary wind
    rocks the lotus-laden water;
The heavy rain
    strikes the wall that's vined.

Dense are the trees on the mountain ridge
    blocking a thousand-mile view;
Like entrails, the rivers twist and wind.

We've all come to Bai Yue[1] where
    the people have tattooed bodies:
Blocked off from letters and news,
    we're each stuck in a village assigned.

登柳州城樓
寄漳汀封連四州刺史

柳宗元 (773 — 819)

城上高樓接大荒，
海天愁思正茫茫。

驚風亂颭芙蓉水，
密雨斜侵薜荔牆。

嶺樹重遮千里目，
江流曲似九迴腸。

共來百越文身地，
猶自音書滯一鄉。

1 In Tang Dynasty, Bai Yue referred to southern China including the present-day Guangdong, Guangxi and Yunnan Provinces which were then not yet developed. These regions were hot and humid and occupied by savage tribes who spoke different languages, had strange customs and tattooed bodies. Northerners considered these places uncivilized and called the people there southern savages (南蠻).

Background:
The poet and his four friends were banished to five different regions in the south in A.D. 815 for their involvement in a failed reform attempt headed by Wang Shuwen (王叔文). The poet himself was banished to Liuzhou, a town in today's Guangxi Province.

THE SONG OF A CHASTE WIFE

Zhang Ji (768 — 830?)

節婦吟

張籍 (768 — 830?)

I've a husband, you well know:
Yet on me
　　　a pair of brilliant pearls you did bestow.

Touched by your tenderness,
On my red silken vest them I did sew.

My home's in a tall house –
　　　above the Imperial garden it rears;
My husband's on duty in the Palace –
　　　he's armed with spears.

I know your heart is pure –
　　　like the sun and the moon...
Yet to marriage vows till death a wife adheres.

These brilliant pearls I return to you in tears:
How regrettable
　　　we didn't meet in my maiden years!

君知妾有夫，
贈妾雙明珠。

感君纏綿意，
繫在紅羅襦。

妾家高樓連宛起，
良人執戟明光裏。

知君用心如日月，
事夫誓擬同生死。

還君明珠雙淚垂，
恨不相逢未嫁時。

AUTUMN THOUGHTS

Zhang Ji (768 — 830?)

秋思

張籍 (768 — 830?)

In Luoyang City,
    howling the autumn winds start;
Home I wish to write
    but countless thoughts fill my heart.

For fear of not speaking
    all my mind in a hurry,
My letter again I unseal
    just before the messenger is to depart.

洛陽城裏見秋風，
欲作家書意萬重。

復恐匆匆說不盡，
行人臨發又開封。

Background:
The poet was a court official posted in Luoyang City, Henan Province, many hundred miles away from his home in Suzhou (蘇州) , Jiangsu Province. He felt homesick when he saw (or more precisely, heard) autumn wind started to howl meaning that autumn had come and the end of the year was near. Traditionally people away from home usually missed their families more towards the end of the year.

YEARNING

Wang Wei (701 — 761)

相思

王維 (701 — 761)

Red beans grow in River South.
How many would sprout in spring?

I wish you'd pick more, my dear friend:
The closest bond they would bring.

紅豆生南國，
春來發幾枝。

願君多採擷，
此物最相思。

Thinking of My Brothers in Shandong on the Ninth Day of the Ninth Month

Wang Wei (701 — 761)

九月九日憶山東兄弟

王維（701 — 761）

Alone in a foreign land, I'm a stranger:
On all festivals,
    longing thoughts for my family overflow.

I know from afar,
    my brothers are climbing the heights,
All wearing dogwood[1] sprays
    but one doesn't show.

獨在異鄉為異客，
每逢佳節倍思親。

遙知兄弟登高處，
遍插茱萸少一人。

---

1 A plant with strong scent. People used to wear or insert its small branches in many places to repel evil spirits according to an old custom.

AN ENVOY AT THE FRONTIER

Wang Wei (701 — 761)

使至塞上

王維（701 — 761）

In my light carriage, an expedition
    to the border I was to mount.
To reach the new protectorate,
    Juyan[1] I had to go around.

Out of the Han frontier,
    I rolled like tumbleweed;
Into the barbarian sky[2],
    I went like a wild goose homeward bound.

In the vast desert,
    a lone pillar of smoke was straight;
Over the long river[3], the setting sun round.

At the Xiao Pass[4] a scout cavalry reported
The Viceroy was in the Yanran[5] battleground.

單車欲問邊，
屬國過居延。

征蓬出漢塞，
歸雁入胡天。

大漠孤煙直，
長河落日圓。

蕭關逢候騎，
都護在燕然。

1　Name of a place in Outer Mongolia.
2　The poet felt he was travelling like tumbleweed and a wild goose on a long journey into Turfan territory outside the west border.
3　The Shiyang River running pass Liangzhou (涼州) towards the north of the desert.
4　One of the ancient pass near the northeastern border.
5　Name of a place in Gansu near Mongolia where a fierce battle was just fought between the Tang army and the Turfans (吐蕃人) .

Background:
In the spring of A.D. 737, the Tang army defeated the Turbans in Wu Wei (武威) (in today's Gansu Province). Turban thus became a protectorate of the Tang Dynasty. The poet, appointed by the Emperor as an envoy, travelled beyond the border to the new protectorate state in Hexi (河西), (now west of Qing Hai Province) in summer of the same year.

Autumn Night in a Mountain Lodge

Wang Wei (701 — 761)

In the empty mountain after a fresh rain,
Autumn's in the air as night begins its reign.

Between the pines,
　　the bright moon shines;
Off the stones,
　　the clear spring waters drain.

The bamboos rustle
　　as clothe-washing girls return;
The lotuses sway
　　as fishing boats down the river plane.

Never mind the passing of the fragrant season,
It's worth for my prince friend here to remain.

山居秋暝

王維〔701 — 761〕

空山新雨後，
天氣晚來秋。

明月松間照，
清泉石上流。

竹喧歸浣女，
蓮動下漁舟。

隨意春芳歇，
王孫自可留。

SEEING PREFECT LI
OFF TO ZIZHOU

Wang Wei (701 — 761)

送梓州李使君

王維（701 — 761）

In ten thousand vales,
      trees soar to the sky;
Through a thousand hills,
      resounds the cuckoo's cry.

In the hills, overnight it rained;
Off the tree-tops, a hundred cascades fly.

As payment for tax, Tong[1] cloths
      the Han[2] women would offer;
To sue over taro fields,
      the Bar[3] people would try.

Like Master Wen[4],
      you'd enlighten the locals,
But on his achievements you won't rely.

萬壑樹參天，
千山響杜鵑。

山中一夜雨，
樹杪百重泉。

漢女輸橦布，
巴人訟芋田。

文翁翻教授，
不敢倚先賢。

---

1 Cloth made from fibres of kapok flowers.

2&3 Local men and women in Zizhou (today's Sichuan Province). Mountains in Sichuan were generally known as Bar mountains (巴山) and local people Bar people (巴人) in ancient times.

4 Wen Weng, a renowned Governor of Su (i.e. Sichuan) in the Han Dynasty. Wen succeeded in providing training to the locals in the backward district and had turned many into scholars and officials of the court.

Background:
Prefect Li was on his way to govern Zizhou (梓州). This place was scenic but very backward in Tang Dynasty. He was expected to deal with the problems among the local tribesmen of different cultures.

BIRD-SINGING BROOK

Wang Wei (701 — 761)

I'm at leisure as cassia flowers fall;
Still is the night
    in the empty mountain of spring.

The rising moon
    startles mountain birds:
At times, by the spring brook they sing.

鳥鳴澗

王維（701 — 761）

人閒桂花落，
夜靜春山空。

月出驚山鳥，
時鳴春澗中。

HIBISCUS BASIN

Wang Wei (701 — 761)

辛夷塢

王維 (701 — 761)

Red hibiscus by the hillside
Bloom brightly on the treetop.

木末芙蓉花，
山中發紅萼。

Silent and desolate is the cabin by the brook;
One after another, the flowers bloom and drop.

澗戶寂無人，
紛紛開且落。

The Song of Wei City

(Farewell to an Ambassador to the West)

Wang Wei (701 — 761)

The light dust has settled in Wei City[1]
    after a morning rain;
Sparkling green is our inn,
    as freshness the willows regain.

I urge you, my dear friend:
    finish another cup of wine:
Westwards beyond Yang Guan[2],
    no friends can be seen again!

渭城曲

（送元二使安西）

王維 （701 — 761）

渭城朝雨浥輕塵，
客舍青青柳色新。

勸君更盡一杯酒，
西出陽關無故人。

---

1 A city near the northwestern border in ancient China in today's Xi'an city, Shaanxi Province.

2 Yang Quan or Yang Pass was situated in the southwest of Dunhuang, Gansu Province on the northwestern border. It was a main western border pass in ancient China.

MY RETREAT AT ZHONGNAN HILL

Wang Wei (701 — 761)

終南別業

王維（701 — 761）

In middle age, I was fascinated with Taoism;
In old age, at the foot of
    Zhongnan Hill my home lies.

When in high spirits,
    often I wander about on my own:
Such joys only I'd realize.

To the end of the water I'd walk,
And sit watching the clouds rise.

By chance I'd meet
    an old fellow of the woods:

We'd chat and laugh
    forgetting to go home as time flies.

中歲頗好道，
晚家南山陲。

興來每獨往，
勝事空自知。

行到水窮處，
坐看雲起時。

偶然值林叟，
談笑無還期。

UNTITLED

Wang Wei (701 — 761)

雜詩

王維〔701 — 761〕

You've come from my home village, sir,
Matters in my home village you should know.

Outside the carved window
    on the day you left,
Had the plum-blossoms started to show?

君自故鄉來，
應知故鄉事。

來日綺窗前，
寒梅著花未？

GREEN BROOK

Wang Wei (701 — 761)

青谿

王維（701 — 761）

To get to the Yellow Flower River,
One often follows the Green Brook.

言入黃花川，
每逐青谿水。

The road winds around mountains for
Scarcely a hundred li[1] with ten thousand crooks.

隨山將萬轉，
趣途無百里。

The waters roar among jumbled rocks,
But serenity is found deep in the pine nook.

聲喧亂石中，
色靜深松裏。

Adrift with water-chestnuts that gently sway,
And mirroring reeds and rushes –
　　　how limpid the waters look!

漾漾泛菱荇，
澄澄映葭葦。

My heart is at peace as ever,
Just like the clear and tranquil brook.

我心素已閒，
清川澹如此。

I wish I could stay on the rocks,
Forever trailing my fishing hook!

請留盤石上，
垂釣將已矣。

1　100 Chinese li is equal to some 30 miles.

FAREWELL (1)

Wang Wei (701 — 761)

We bade farewell to each other in the hills;
I closed the brushwood door at nightfall.

The grass turns green
    in spring year after year:
Would you my prince friend again call?

送別 （1）

王維（701 — 761）

山中相送罷，
日暮掩柴扉。

春草年年綠，
王孫歸不歸。

FAREWELL (2)

Wang Wei (701 — 761)

Dismounted from my horse,
      I offered you a drink,
And asked where you would go.

You said you couldn't achieve your goal:
Return you would to the foot of
      the Southern Mountain[1] and lie low.

You're gone and I hear of you no more —
Endlessly, white clouds drift to and fro[2].

1&2 Living as a recluse in the country far away from worldly affairs but close to nature under white clouds
    was regarded as good virtue especially among scholars in the old days. Southern Mountain was also
    called the Zhong Nan Mountain (終南山) .

送別 （2）

王維（701 — 761）

下馬飲君酒，
問君何所之。

君言不得意，
歸臥南山陲。

但去莫復聞，
白雲無盡時。

BAMBOO GROVE

Wang Wei (701 — 761)

竹里館

王維 (701 — 761)

Alone in a secluded bamboo grove I sit,
Playing the qin[1] and chanting free.

Deep in the forest where no one knows,
Comes the bright moon to shine on me.

獨坐幽篁裏，
彈琴復長嘯。

深林人不知，
明月來相照。

1 Guqin (古琴) — an ancient 7-stringed musical instrument looking like a pedal steel guitar.

DEER ENCLOSURE

Wang Wei (701 — 761)

鹿柴

王維（701 — 761）

Not a soul is seen in the empty mountain,
But I hear people's voice echoes.

Sunlight sneaks through the dense wood,
And the green moss glows.

空山不見人，
但聞人語響。

返景入深林，
復照青苔上。

AN OLD MARCHING SONG

Li Qi (Early 8th century)

We climb the hills
  to watch for beacon fires at daylight;
We water our horses
  by the Jiao River at twilight.

The guard strikes the hour
  as a sandstorm brings darkness;
The Princess[1] with her pi-pa
  was once left in a sorry plight.

No city wall's seen for ten thousand miles –
  in the wild only clouds floating atop,
Rain and snow keep pouring down
  mingling with the vast desert non-stop.

Dolefully Tartar geese honk,
  as they fly by night after night;
While the Tartars' tears fall drop by drop.

I heard passage through Jade Pass is still banned[2]:
Warriors must risk their lives
  behind the light chariot in command[3].

Year after year, bones of the fallen
  lie buried in the wild:
Only to have Tartar grapes
  brought to the Palace of Han[4].

古從軍行

李頎 (八世紀初)

白日登山望烽火，黃昏飲馬傍交河。
行人刁斗風沙暗，公主琵琶幽怨多。

野雲萬里無城郭，雨雪紛紛連大漠。
胡雁哀鳴夜夜飛，胡兒眼淚雙雙落。

聞道玉門猶被遮，應將性命逐輕車。
年年戰骨埋野外，空見蒲萄入漢家。

1　A princess of Han Dynasty (B.C. 206 — A.D. 220) was sent to Xinjiang to marry a Tartar prince. A pipa was specially made to accompany her so that she could hear Han music while in the barbarian land.

2　During their expedition to conquer the barbarian land, the Han Emperor decreed that soldiers would not be allowed to cross the Jade Pass (玉門關) for home before their triumph over the Tartars.

3　The army chief took command in a light chariot in ancient times. Warriors fought on foot behind.

4　Han Dynasty (B.C. 206 — A.D. 220).

SEEING OFF CHEN ZHANGFU

Li Qi (Early 8th century)

The barley turns yellow
  as southern winds of the fourth month blow;
Date blossoms are yet to fall
  while lush the Wutong leaves grow.

The blue mountain we left at dawn
  is again seen at eve;
Our horses neighed as we set off
  recalling our homes of long ago.

Sir, how noble is your bearing,
  how broad your mind!
You've curling whiskers and tiger brows
  and your forehead's wide.

Inside your belly,
  ten thousand volumes you keep –
You won't lower yourself in the countryside.

By the east gate, wine for us you used to buy;
Carefree, worldly affairs
  were light as feather to your eye.

Lying drunk, you knew not dusk had come;
At times, you stared blankly
  at the solitary clouds on high.

Rolling waves of the Yellow River
　　　　joined with the darkened sky;
Ferry officials stopped the boats
　　　　suspending river-crossing thereby.

The traveller from Zheng[1] is not yet home:
The guest of Luoyang[2] vainly heaves a sigh.

I heard back home you've many friends,
After quitting your job yesterday,
　　　　what are your plans?

送陳章甫

李頎（八世紀初）

四月南風大麥黃，棗花未落桐葉長。
青山朝別暮還見，嘶馬出門思故鄉。

陳侯立身何坦蕩，虬鬚虎眉仍大顙。
腹中貯書一萬卷，不肯低頭在草莽。

東門酤酒飲我曹，心輕萬事皆鴻毛，
醉臥不知白日暮，有時空望孤雲高。

長河浪高連天黑，津吏停舟渡不得。
鄭國遊人未及家，洛陽行子空嘆息。

聞道故林相識多，罷官昨日今如何？

1　Ancient kingdom of Zheng (鄭國) in today's Hebei Province from where his friend Chen Zhangfu came.
2　A city in northern China in Henan Province where the poet was staying as a guest.

GRIEF OF SEPARATION

Yuan Zhen (779 — 831)

離思

元積 (779 — 831)

No water is comparable to the green sea;
No cloud to the clouds of Mt Wu[1].

No woman is worthy of my backward glance:
Partly due to ascetic practice, partly you.

曾經滄海難為水，
除卻巫山不是雲。

取次花叢懶回顧，
半緣修道半緣君。

---

1 A mountain in the Three Gorges along the Yangtze River near Chongqing in Sichuan Province. It is well-known for its legendary twelve peaks.

Background:
The poet wrote this poem in commemoration of his dead wife whom he deeply loved and missed.

LONGING IN SPRING

Huangfu Ran (718 — 771)

春思

皇甫冉 (718 — 771)

A new year's announced
　　　as swallows chatter and orioles cry –
But thousands of miles away
　　　Ma-yi and Long-du[1] lie.

My home's in the capital
　　　next to the Imperial Garden of Han[2] –
But my heart has gone with the moon
　　　to the barbarian sky.

The brocade poems[3]
　　　reveal everlasting regret;
Flowers laugh at me
　　　as I sleep alone on high.

I'd ask General Dou of the cavalry,
When will victory be carved on Mt Yanran[4]
　　　and the homecoming banners fly?

鶯啼燕語報新年，
馬邑龍堆路幾千。

家往層城鄰漢苑，
心隨明月到胡天。

機中錦字論長恨，
樓上花枝笑獨眠。

為問元戎竇車騎，
何時返旆勒燕然？

1　Places on the northwest border near Xinjiang where the Tang army was fighting the invading Turfans (吐蕃人).

2　Han Dynasty B.C. 206 — A.D. 220 .

3　A famous love poem woven into brocade by Su Hui of the Jin Dynasty (A.D. 265 — A.D. 420) and sent to her husband in the frontier. It consists of some 800 characters that made many perfect poems even when read from a reversed direction (迴文詩).

4　A mountain in Gansu near Inner Mongolia where the Turfans were defeated by the Tang army after a fierce battle details of which were carved on a rock in commemoration of the victory. Here the poet indirectly asked when her husband would return from the frontier battlefield.

CHRYSANTHEMUM (1)

Huang Chao (820 — 884)

Braving the bitter west wind,
　　all over the garden you unfold;
Butterflies won't come
　　as your stamens and aroma are cold.

Should I become God of Spring one day,
To bloom with peach flowers you'd be told.

題菊花 （1）

黃巢 （820 — 884）

颯颯西風滿院栽，
蕊寒香冷蝶難來。

他年我若為青帝，
報與桃花一處開。

CHRYSANTHEMUM (2)

Huang Chao (820 — 884)

Wait till autumn comes
　　on the eighth of October[1];
My flowers[2] will bloom –
　　then all other flowers will be over.

Sweet scent will shoot through
　　the sky of Chang'an[3]:
The city will be packed with
　　golden armour[4] shoulder to shoulder.

題菊花 （2）

黃巢（820 — 884）

待到秋來九月八，
我花開後百花殺。

衝天香陣透長安，
滿城盡是黃金甲。

1　The ninth month on the lunar calendar equates approximately to October.

2　Chrysanthemum, the writer's favourite flower.

3　The capital of Tang Dynasty.

4　The bright yellow chrysanthemum was likened to the golden armour worn by elite soldiers in ancient times. The poet hinted his soldiers would take over the city in October.

Background:
The writer of this poet failed in the state examination and was extremely upset. He later joined the peasant rebellion and became its leader. The rebels defeated the Tang Imperial army and he successfully established his own short-lived kingdom in Chang'an in A.D. 880. He was defeated four years later and killed himself in A.D. 884.

REMINISCENCE IN A TOWER

Zhao Gu (806 — 853)

江樓感舊

趙嘏 (806 — 853)

In solitude and bemused,
    a riverside tower climb I;
The moonlight's like water,
    the water's like the sky.

Where's my moon-admiring companion?
The scene vaguely
    resembles last year's to my eye.

獨上江樓思渺然，
月光如水水如天。

同來望月人何處，
風景依稀似去年。

QING MING FESTIVAL

Du Mu (803 — 852)

It rained at Qing Ming Festival[1] all day,
Wayfarers were filled with dismay.

Asked where a wine bar was,
A shepherd boy pointed to
    the Apricot Village[2] faraway.

清明

杜牧 (803 — 852)

清明時節雨紛紛，
路上行人欲斷魂。

借問酒家何處有，
牧童遙指杏花村。

---

1 A Chinese festival in April when all people pay visits to their ancestors' graves.

2 An old village now in Anhui Province.

SPRING IN RIVER SOUTH

Du Mu (803 — 852)

江南春絕句

杜牧（803 — 852）

For a thousand miles,
    orioles sing amid patches of red and green;
Waterfront and hillside villages are strewn
    with wine banners fluttering in between.

Four hundred and eighty temples
    have been there since the South Dynasty[1];
In the mist and rain,
    many pagodas and towers can still be seen.

千里鶯啼綠映紅，
水村山郭酒旗風。

南朝四百八十寺，
多少樓台煙雨中。

---

1 Emperors in the South Dynasty (A.D. 420 — A.D. 479) were devoted Buddhists. A large number of temples were built during this period. These emperors were all gone, only the temples remained in the River South.

MOORED AT QINHUAI

Du Mu (803 — 852)

夜泊秦淮

杜牧 (803 — 852)

The mist veiled the chilly water and
    the moon veils the sandbar;
By night at Qinhuai River,
    we moored near a wine bar.

Oblivious of the sorrows of a kingdom lost,
Across the river, a sing-song girl
    is still singing the lyric Hou Ting Hua[1].

煙籠寒水月籠沙，
夜泊秦淮近酒家。

商女不知忘國恨，
隔江猶唱後庭花。

---

1 A lyric written by Emperor Chen Hou Zhu of the Chen State (A.D. 557 — A.D. 589) for his beloved
concubine and was regarded as an inauspicious song. Chen lost his kingdom through his indulgence in
women and pleasure seeking.

Background:
Du Mu's boat moored by the Qinhuai River (秦淮河) in a misty moonlit night. The song as sung by
a sing-song girl alarmed him and reminded him of the situation of the current Tang Emperor who had
also become indulgent in women and pleasure seeking. As a result the Tang Dynasty was weakening year
after year. He worried that the Tang Emperor could have a similar fate.

PUTTING ONE'S MIND AT EASE

Du Mu (803 — 852)

遺懷

杜牧 (803 — 852)

Dejected, with wine I roamed far and wide;
Slim was the waist of the Chu[1] girl
    who on one's palm could ride.

From this ten-year-long dream
    of Yangzhou I awake,
Only to find 'the heart-breaker
    of the blue chambers'[2] to my name is tied.

落魄江湖載酒行，
楚腰纖細掌中輕。

十年一覺揚州夢，
贏得青樓薄倖名。

---

1 Girls from the Kingdom of Chu in the north were famous for being slim and excellent dancers. They danced before guests during dinners. The legend says some were so light that they could even dance in a man's palm. In those days, the Emperor of Chu loved slim waists. Consequently, many girls in the palace were starved to death (楚王好細腰，宮中多餓死。).

2 Blue chambers in those days referred to the houses of courtesans.

RED CLIFF[1]

Du Mu (803 — 852)

赤壁

杜牧（803 — 852）

Broken halberds lie buried in the sand
    but their iron parts still remain;
I have them washed and polished –
    they bear witness to a former reign.

Had the east wind not helped
    Admiral Zhou[2],
To the Bronze Bird Terrace[3] deep in spring,
    the two Qiao's[4] would have been chained.

折戟沉沙鐵未銷，
自將磨洗認前朝。

東風不與周郎便，
銅雀春深鎖二喬。

1 Located along the Yangtze River near the Three Gorges in Chongqing City, the Red Cliff was the site of a famous battle in the East Han Dynasty (A.D. 25 — A.D. 220) in which Zhou Yu (周瑜) (A.D. 175 — A.D. 210) commander of the allied forces of Wu and Shu, torched the fleet of Cao Cao (曹操) (A.D. 155 — A.D. 220) in the year 208.

2 Zhou Yu, commander of the allied force of Wu and Shu in the battle of the Red Cliff.

3 Bronze Bird Terrace (銅雀臺) was a secret pleasure palace of Cao Cao (曹操) now in Henan Province. Had Zhou Yu lost the battle, his wife and sister-in-law (大喬及小喬) would both be taken by Cao and locked up in the Terrace for his own enjoyment.

4 These were the two beautiful sisters known as big Qiao and small Qiao (大喬及小喬). They were the wives of Sun Ce (東吳國主孫策即孫權兄) and Zhou Yu (周瑜) respectively.

AUTUMN EVENING

Du Mu (803 — 852)

秋夕

杜牧 (803 — 852)

By the cold painted screen, silvery candles
    flicker in autumn moonlight.
She hits at drifting fireflies,
    with a silken fan small and light.

Cool as water is the night by the palace steps;
She lies down and both the Cowherd
    and Weaver Girl[1] come in sight.

銀燭秋光冷畫屏，
輕羅小扇撲流螢。

天階夜色涼如水，
臥看牽牛織女星。

---

1 Two stars positioned on either side of the Milky Way. Chinese legend has it that they are heavenly lovers. But the couple can only meet once a year on the night of the 7th day of the 7th lunar month when countless magpies would form a bridge to enable them to meet across the Milky Way. This particular day is also known as Chinese Lovers' Day.

Background:
This poem depicts a scene in which a young, naive and lonesome concubine in the palace on the night of the Chinese Lovers' Day, was dreaming of love.

THE GOLDEN VALLEY GARDEN[1]

Du Mu (803 — 852)

金谷園

杜牧 (803 — 852)

Along with the fragrant dust[2],
    gone are the glories and luxurious life.
How heartless the water continues to flow,
    the grass continues to thrive!

Birds lament in the east wind at dusk;
Falling flowers look like someone
    from the tower making a death dive[3].

繁華事散逐香塵，
流水無情草自春。

日暮東風怨啼鳥，
落花猶似墜樓人。

1　An extremely luxurious garden residence built by a super-rich man named Shi Chong (石崇) in the Jin Dynasty (晉朝 A.D. 265 — A.D. 420) .

2　Fine particles (or dust) of eaglewood or aloes wood (沉香) .　Shi Chong had his dancing girls practised dancing on a platform made of ivory on which fine particles of the expensive wood were sprinkled thus filling the entire hall with fragrance.　Such luxury ended after Shi was arrested.

3　Shi had a beautiful dancing girl call Lu Zhu (綠珠) whom he loved.　Sun Xiu (孫秀) , a powerful court official who was fond of Lu Zhu, asked to take possession of her but Shi refused.　Sun framed Shi up for treason and had him arrested.　Lu Zhu was sad his master was ruined because of her.　She jumped from the tower to her death on the date of Shi's arrest.

SIGHING OVER A FLOWER

Du Mu (803 — 852)

嘆花

杜牧 (803 — 852)

It's too late to look for one's favourite flower –
Despair and complain not,
    having missed the finest hour.

What's left is a green shady tree full of fruits:
The violent wind has ripped away
    all its crimson colour.

自是尋春去校遲，
不須惆悵怨芳時。

狂風落盡深紅色，
綠樹成陰子滿枝。

FAREWELL (1)

Du Mu (803 — 852)

At just over thirteen,
    you're elegant and cute:
Like a nutmeg bud on a twig
    in the primrose season new.

For ten miles along the streets of Yangzhou
    in the spring breeze,
Roll up all the beaded curtains —
    no prettier girls would come into view.

贈別 （Ⅰ）

杜牧（803 — 852）

娉娉裊裊十三餘，
豆蔻枝頭二月初。

春風十里揚州路，
捲上珠簾總不如。

FAREWELL (2)

Du Mu (803 — 852)

Deeply in love but
      our passion appears to have gone;
Before the wine, no smile we don.

The candle has a heart[1] —
      it grieves to see us part,
And sheds tears[2] for us till dawn.

贈別 （2）

杜牧 (803 — 852)

多情卻似總無情，
唯覺樽前笑不成。

蠟燭有心還惜別，
替人垂淚到天明。

---

1 The wick of a candle. The Chinese word for 'wick' is (燭心) which literally means 'heart of the candle'.
2 Molten wax that drips along a candle while burning is likened to tears shed on the face when one weeps.

PASSING BY HUA QING PALACE

過華清宮

Du Mu (803 — 852)

杜牧 (803 — 852)

The palace clusters of Chang'an[1]
    look glorious to my backward glance;
Thousands of doors
    on the peak open one by one.

The galloping courier is greeted by
    the smile of the Concubine[2]:
The arrival of Lychees[3] is known to none!

長安回望繡成堆，
山頂千門次第開。

一騎紅塵妃子笑，
無人知是荔枝來。

1 The capital in Tang Dynasty.

2 Yang Gui Fei (楊貴妃). The legendary beloved concubine of Emperor Tang Xuan Zong (唐玄宗).

3 A delicate and delicious fruit available only in Guangdong Province in southern China during a very brief period in summer each year. The fruit has to be eaten fresh within days or it would rot.

Background:
Lychees were the favourite fruit of Yang Gui Fei. In those days, lychees were delivered by horses galloping non-stop day and night all the way from Guangdong to the palace in order to keep them fresh. The poet hinted that the Emperor, by instructing their delivery thousands of miles from the capital, went to the extreme to please his concubine.

A LETTER TO HAN CHUO, PREFECT OF YANGZHOU

Du Mu (803 — 852)

寄揚州韓綽判官

杜牧（803 — 852）

Dim, dim is the blue mountain
　　beyond the water far, far away.

Autumn is gone in River South
　　but grasses are yet to decay.

With a flute by the Twenty-four Bridge[1]
　　in the moonlight,

Where do the beauties teach you to play?

青山隱隱水迢迢，
秋盡江南草未凋。

二十四橋明月夜，
玉人何處教吹簫。

---

1 Name of a famous bridge in Yangzhou so named because of a legend that 24 immortal beauties once played flutes together on it in ancient times.

ASCENDING THE STORK TOWER [1]

Wang Zhihuan (688 — 742)

Behind the mountains,
      the white sun vanishes;
Into the sea, the Yellow River flows.

For the farthest thousand-mile view,
Up another level, one goes.

1 The Stork Tower was situated in the southwest of today's
Pu County (蒲縣) in Shanxi Province.

登鸛雀樓

王之渙（688 — 742）

白日依山盡，
黃河入海流。

欲窮千里目，
更上一層樓。

BEYOND THE FRONTIER

Wang Zhihuan (688 — 742)

出塞

王之渙 (688 — 742)

The Yellow River climbs
    to the white clouds, far, far away;
Amid towering mountains,
    a solitary city[1] stays.

Why should the Tartar flute play
    "Bemoaning the Willows"[2].
Never would the spring breezes
    cross the Yu Men Gateway[3].

黃河遠上白雲間，
一片孤城萬仞山。

羌笛何須怨楊柳，
春風不度玉門關。

1 The old city of Lanzhou in Wuwei County (武威縣), Gansu Province. This was a frontier city in Tang Dynasty.

2 The name of this tune was amended from a popular tune in ancient China called "Breaking the Willows" (折楊柳) to reflect the resentment of the soldiers who were kept in the outpost far too long.

3 Border gate at northwest frontier in ancient China, now in west Dunhuang in Gansu Province. It was also known as Jade Pass beyond which is today's Xinjiang Uygur Autonomous Region. The Han Emperor had decreed that soldiers stationed in the frontier were not allowed to pass through Yu Men Gateway without his permission.

AT A FAREWELL DINNER

Wang Zhihuan (688 — 742)

The spring water by the bank
	is green and running slow;
Into the Zhang River it'd flow.

Never mind the repeated calls to set sail:
The Peach Stream's still too shallow to row.

宴詞

王之渙（688 — 742）

長堤春水綠悠悠，
畎入漳河一道流。

莫聽聲聲催去棹，
桃溪淺處不勝舟。

A WARRIOR'S PLAINT

Liu Zhongyong (year of birth and death unknown)

征人怨

柳中庸（生卒年不詳）

Year after year, patrolling
　　the Golden River[1] and Gate of Jade[2];
Morning after morning, cracking
　　the whip and wielding the blade.

To Zhao Jun's[3] tomb,
　　the snow of spring returns;
Circling Black Mount[4], a ten-thousand-mile
　　journey the Yellow River[5] has made.

歲歲金河復玉關，
朝朝馬策與刀環。

三春白雪歸青塚，
萬里黃河繞黑山。

1&4　Now in Inner Mongolia.

2　Also known as Yu Men Gateway or Yu Men Guan, see previous notes.

3　Princess Wang Zhaojun's tomb (王昭君墓), now in the city of Huhot (呼和浩特) in Inner Mongolia.

5　Regarded by Chinese as a symbol of motherland. Here the poet showed his longing for motherland which was ten thousand miles away.

WOMAN ROCK[1]

Wang Jian (766 — 813)

Where she looked out for her husband,
A river runs endlessly as ever.
Turned into a rock:
Return she could never.

Day after day on the hill,
　　the wind and the rain beat:
When the traveller returns,
　　him the rock would greet.

望夫石

王建（766 — 813）

望夫處，江悠悠。
化為石，不回頭。

山頭日日風復雨，
行人歸來石應語。

1　The legend has it that the woman's husband was summoned to work on the construction of the Great Wall in the Qin Dynasty (B.C. 221 — B.C.206) and never returned. She stood waiting by a river day after day for so long that eventually she turned into a woman-shape rock. There are quite a number of such rocks by the side of rivers in northern China.

PLAINT OF SPRING

Liu Fangping (year of birth and death unkown)

春怨

劉方平（生卒年不詳）

Outside the gauze window,
　　the sun's setting, twilight drawing near.
Inside a golden house[1],
　　no one sees the stain of her tear.

Desolate is the yard
　　as spring is on the wane;
Doors are not opened –
　　spread all over are flowers of the pear.

紗窗日落漸黃昏，
金屋無人見淚痕。

寂寞空庭春欲晚，
梨花滿地不開門。

1　A golden house was a place in which a rich man kept his mistress.

SPRING DREAM

Cen Shen (715 — 779)

春夢

岑參〈715 — 779〉

Last night, into our bridal room
　　a spring breeze blew:
You're faraway by the Xiang River –
　　oh how I missed you!

A moment on the pillow in a spring dream,
Thousands of miles
　　in River South I roamed through.

洞房昨夜春風起，
遙憶美人湘江水。

枕上片時春夢中，
行盡江南數千里。

ON MEETING AN ENVOY RETURNING TO THE CAPITAL

Cen Shen (715 — 779)

逢入京使

岑參 (715 — 779)

East towards home, the road stretches
　　on and on before my eyes;
My sleeves tremble and are
　　wet with tear that never dries.

On horseback we meet
　　without paper and brush[1]:
To tell my family I'm safe and well,
　　on you, your friend relies.

故園東望路漫漫，
雙袖龍鍾淚不乾。

馬上相逢無紙筆，
憑君傳語報平安。

1　A brush and a pot of ink were used to write in ancient China before the pen was invented. The poet was in the frontier thousands of miles away from home. He asked a friend who was returning to the capital to bring a verbal message to his home.

THE DONG TING LAKE

題龍陽縣青草湖

Tang Wenru (8th Century)

唐温如 (八世紀)

The west wind
    blew Dong Ting's youthful face away[1];
Overnight,
    the Xiang traveller's[2] hair turned grey.
Drunk, he knows not
    the sky is afloat in the water;
A boat laden with sweet dreams
    weighs down the Milky Way.

西風吹老洞庭波，
一夜湘君白髮多。

醉後不知天在水，
滿船清夢壓星河。

---

1 The smooth surface of the lake was wrinkled by the west wind.
2 A traveller from Sichuan. Here it means the poet himself.

A GUEST IN WUSHAN[1]

Cui Tu (Late 9th century)

Five thousand miles away,
　　I've been a guest for three years;
Before the twelve peaks[2],
　　autumn hues are on show.

A soul totally lost
　　upon parting can't be recalled:
The sun's setting in the west,
　　the waters eastward flow.

巫山旅別

崔塗（九世紀末）

五千里外三年客，
十二峯前一望秋。

無限別魂招不得，
夕陽西下水東流。

1　A mountain in the Three Gorges along the Yangtze River near Chongqing in Sichuan Province.

2　The famous and legendary twelve peaks of Wushan.

ASCENDING THE LEYOU PLATEAU[1]

Li Shangyin (813 — 858)

登樂遊原

李商隱 (813 — 858)

Feeling restless in the evening,
Towards the ancient plateau a carriage I steer.

The sunset is magnificent —
But dusk is near.

向晚意不適，
驅車登古原。

夕陽無限好，
只是近黃昏。

---

1 On the southeast edge of the old capital, Chang'an (now Xi'an). It was the highest point commending an excellent view of the city.

UNTITLED (1)

Li Shangyin (813 — 858)

Hard it was to meet you –
　　hard as well to say goodbye.
The east wind's powerless[1], all flowers die.

Only when a spring silk-worm perishes,
　　would its silk be exhausted;
Only when a candle burns to ashes,
　　would its tears[2] dry.

At dawn by the mirror,
　　you'd worry your hair may change;
By night reciting poems,
　　you'd feel the moonlight's chill above high.

The Penglai Mount[3] is not far from here:
Green bird[4], to look for her please diligently try.

無題 （１）

李商隱（813 — 858）

相見時難別亦難，
東風無力百花殘。

春蠶到死絲方盡，
蠟炬成灰淚始乾。

曉鏡但愁雲鬢改，
夜吟應覺月光寒。

蓬山此去無多路，
青鳥殷勤為探看。

1　East wind blows in spring in northern China. When it becomes powerless, spring had gone and flowers would wither. This line reflected the sorrowful mind of the poet.

2　Molten wax that drips along a candle while burning is likened to teardrops that fall along the face when one weeps.

3　A fairyland in the East Sea according to the legend. Here the poet imagined his lover lived in a fairyland.

4　According to the legend, the green bird was believed to be a convoy of the Goddess of the West (西王母). Here the poet, in despair, was hoping it might help him to find his lover.

UNTITLED (2)

Li Shangyin (813 — 858)

無題 （2）

李商隱 （813 — 858）

The stars of last night–
  the breezes of last night–
By the west of the painted tower
  and east of the Cassia Hall site.

Phoenix's wings we lacked,
  to fly as a pair,
But linked were our hearts
  by the rhino horn's magical might[1].

Apart we sat in the 'fishing game'[2]
  enjoying warm spring wine;
In groups we divided playing at riddles[2]
  under the red lantern light.

How sad I had to report duty,
  on hearing the drum-beats[3],
Riding to the Orchid Terrace[4],
  I was like thistledown in flight!

昨夜星辰昨夜風，
畫樓西畔桂堂東。

身無彩鳳雙飛翼，
心有靈犀一點通。

隔座送鈎春酒暖，
分曹射覆蠟燈紅。

嗟余聽鼓應官去，
走馬蘭臺類轉蓬。

1   According to the legend, a line runs through the rhino's horn from tip to end thus it was believed to have a magical power to spiritually connect two persons in love.

2   Popular games at dinner table in the Tang Dynasty.

3   Drumbeats from the drum tower signalled time in ancient days. Here it signified dawn was near after a feast and an overnight stay in a stately mansion and the poet had to report duty for a new posting.

4   This was the Court Secretariat where the poet would be assigned a new post. The poet felt sad having to leave the current post and the woman he loved. He likened himself to thistledown being blown about in the wind.

UNTITLED (3)

Li Shangyin (813 — 858)

Scented silk curtain embroidered
　　with phoenix tails, flimsy and multi-fold;
Green patterns on a circular canopy
　　deep in the night I saw her sew.

A moon-shaped fan hid not her blush;
A coach thundered by
　　before words from our lips could flow.

Golden candle wicks burn dim
　　in loneliness ever since:
News about her comes not
　　though red the pomegranates grow[1].

My dappled horse is just tethered
　　by the bank of weeping willows –
Where in the southwest
　　would a favourable wind blow?[2]

無題 （3）

李商隱 (813 — 858)

鳳尾香羅薄幾重，
碧文圓頂夜深縫。

扇裁月魄羞難掩，
車走雷聲語未通。

曾是寂寥金燼暗，
斷無消息石榴紅。

斑騅只繫垂楊岸，
何處西南任好風。

1　Pomegranates grow red in the 5th month of the lunar calendar i.e. June in central and northern China. The poet hinted that a year had passed since he met her when she was adorning a new gauze curtain the summer before.

2　The poet hoped he could find a favourable wind that would take him to her place.

UNTITLED (4)

Li Shangyin (813 — 858)

無題 （4）

李商隱 (813 — 858)

Coming is an empty promise:
　　you're gone and nowhere to be found.

The moon slants over the house
　　as the fifth watch bell starts to sound.

Vainly in my dreams,
　　I cried over your departure;

Pale are the words hastily written
　　in ink not well ground[1].

The candle illuminates half cage
　　of gold-threaded kingfisher;

The hibiscus-embroidered curtain
　　releases the scent of musk around.

Master Liu[2] complained
　　Penglai Mount[3] was remote,

But you're ten thousand times
　　farther away from Penglai Mount.

來是空言去絕蹤，
月斜樓上五更鐘。

夢為遠別啼難喚，
書被催成墨未濃。

蠟照半籠金翡翠，
麝熏微度繡芙蓉。

劉郎已恨蓬山遠，
更隔蓬山一萬重。

1　There was no bottled ink in ancient times. Ink had to be prepared by slowing grinding to dissolve an ink bar on a stone pad adding a small amount of water at a time. If the ink was not well ground, the ink did not thicken hence the writing in brush did not look solid.

2　The legend has it that in East Han Dynasty (A.D. 25 — A.D. 220), Liu and his friend met two pretty fairy girls while collecting herbs in a remote mountain near the East Sea called Fenglai (蓬萊). The girls invited them to their homes and they lived together happily for half a year before leaving. They later returned to the mountains to look for the girls but their search was in vain.

3　Penglai Mountain was believed to be inhabited by fairies.

UNTITLED (5)

Li Shangyin (813 — 858)

In the Sorrow-free[1] Chamber,
　　multiple curtains hang low;
Awaken in the silent night,
　　the time's running slow.

The life of the Wushan Goddess[2]
　　was but a dream;
The Blue Brook Maid's[3] abode
　　never does any man know.

The wind and the waves know not
　　water-chestnut flowers are frail;
In the moonlight on dewy cinnamon leaves
　　fragrance who would bestow?

It's useless to speak one's mind;
I regret not if indulgence
　　fills my heart with woe.

無題 （5）

李商隱 (813 — 858)

重帷深下莫愁堂，
臥後清宵細細長。

神女生涯原是夢，
小姑居處本無郎。

風波不信菱枝弱，
月露誰教桂葉香。

直道相思了無益，
未妨惆悵是輕狂。

1　Sorrow-free (莫愁) was the name of a pretty girl in Jinling (金陵) the former name of today's Nanjing. It was later used to indicate a pretty girl friend.

2　Ancient legend has it that Emperor Chu (楚王) once had a secret meeting with the Goddess of Wu Shan (巫山 i.e. the mountain in the Three Gorges near Chonqing) in his dream on a rainy night during his hunting trip in Wu Shan. When the Emperor woke up the next morning, the Goddess could not be found. Only a sharp peak surrounded by clouds was seen. The Emperor was heartbroken. This sharp peak was later called the Goddess Peak (神女峯). It was also known that the Goddess would appear in the form of clouds in the morning and rain at night (旦為朝雲，暮為行雨) and could be met only in a dream.

3　The Blue Brook Maid (青溪小姑), according to the legend, was a talented pretty girl who once lived alone by a secluded blue brook.

CHANG E (Goddess of the Moon)

Li Shangyin (813 — 858)

嫦娥

李商隱 (813 — 858)

On the mother-of-pearl screen,
    deep are the shadows of the candlelight;
Gradually sinking is the Milky Way,
    morning stars fading away from sight.

Chang E[1] should regret
    stealing the elixir of life:
What a lonely heart, amid green seas
    and blue skies, night after night!

雲母屏風燭影深，
長河漸落曉星沉。

嫦娥應悔偷靈药，
碧海青天夜夜心。

1 According to ancient legend, Chang E stole the elixir from her husband and swallowed it. All of a sudden, she became as light as a feather and soon floated out of the window towards the moon and never returned. People believed she had become immortal and was living in the moon.

Jia Sheng[1]

Li Shangyin (813 — 858)

The Emperor summoned banished officials
　　looking for people with flair.
Jia's talents were beyond compare.

What a pity – having been given
　　the front seat in the middle of the night,
He was asked about ghosts and spirits
　　but not the people's welfare.

賈生

李商隱（813 — 858）

宣室求賢訪逐臣，
賈生才調更無倫。

可憐夜半虛前席，
不問蒼生問鬼神。

1　Jia Sheng, or Jia Yi (賈誼), a talented courtier in Han Dynasty (B.C. 206 — A.D. 220) whose submissions upset the Emperor and was banished to Chang Sha (長沙) for three years. He was called to the palace for advice one year after his exile. The poet deplored the Emperor's concern on ghosts and gods rather than the livelihood of the people.

THE ORNATE ZITHER

Li Shangyin (813 — 858)

錦瑟

李商隱 (813 — 858)

For no reason,
  the ornate zither has fifty strings;
Each string with its fret
  evokes recollection of a youthful spring.

Zhuangzi[1] was baffled
  by his dawn dream of being a butterfly;
The cuckoo was entrusted
  with the tender soul of a king[2].

In the green sea under a bright moon,
  tears would turn into pearls[3];
In Lantian under a warm sun,
  rising mists the jade would bring[4].

Such feeling may be left to memories –
Only at the time it was a puzzling thing.

錦瑟無端五十絃，
一絃一柱思華年。

莊生曉夢迷蝴蝶，
望帝春心托杜鵑。

滄海月明珠有淚，
藍田日暖玉生煙。

此情可待成追憶，
只是當時已惘然。

1　A celebrated Taoist philosopher and scholar who explained his dawn dream: he said he was not sure if he was a man who dreamt of being a butterfly or was he a butterfly having a dream of being a man.

2　King Wang of the ancient Kingdom of Su who was bereaved of his beloved concubine. The legend said he missed her so much that after his death his soul was transformed into a cuckoo the following spring. The cuckoo's sad calls sounded like the king's tender words to his concubine: "why not come home? (不如歸去)" and it wept tears of blood.

3　According to an ancient legend, mermaids would shed tears in grief when the full moon shines and the tears would turn into pearls.

4　Lantian is a mountain in Shaanxi Province which has large deposits of fine jade. Locals in ancient times believed that the jade deposits would attract mists to the mountain when the sun warmed it up.

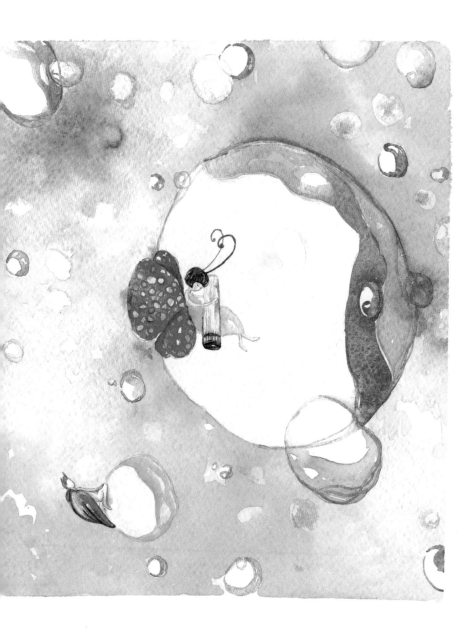

Background:
The poet was coming up to 45 years old at the time and was believed to be making a recount of his romances in life.

FALLEN FLOWERS

Li Shangyin (813 — 858)

After all, the guest[1] of the tower has left:
Petals in the small garden fly in disarray.

Unevenly they heap all over the winding path,
Bidding farewell to the slanting sun far away.

Heart-broken, I can't bear to sweep them off:
Eagerly gazing, I still wish return she may.

Gone is my tender heart with spring,
Wetting my coat with tears on its way.

落花

李商隱 (813 — 858)

高閣客竟去，
小園花亂飛。

參差連曲陌，
迢遞送斜輝。

腸斷未忍掃，
眼穿仍欲歸。

芳心向春盡，
所得是沾衣。

---

1   It was believed that the poet's 'guest of the tower' was in fact Spring. He was sad Spring had left before his very eyes and wished she might return.

SPRING RAIN

Li Shangyin (813 — 858)

春雨

李商隱 (813 — 858)

Dressed in white in new spring[1],
    dispirited I lie….
White Gate[2] is desolate,
    my plan has gone awry.

In the rain, the red mansion[3] looked cold;
Behind the beaded curtain
    in flickering lamplight[4], alone returned I.

How sad the spring sun
    was sinking during the long trip;
By night's end, faintly in my dream you came by.

How can my letter with jade earrings[5] reach you?
By a wild goose[6] winging its way
    ten thousand miles across the cloudy sky.

悵臥新春白袷衣，
白門寥落意多違。

紅樓隔雨相望冷，
珠箔飄燈獨自歸。

遠路應悲春晼晚，
殘宵猶得夢依稀。

玉璫緘札何由達，
萬里雲羅一雁飛。

1　The period between the 10th day and the 20th day after the Chinese New Year day was known as 'new spring' in ancient times.

2　Name of a place where the poet was known to have a love affair. Some said it was somewhere near today's city of Nanjing.

3　The house where the poet's lover once lived was deserted when the poet paid a visit to the place in the rain.

4　Inside a carriage.

5　Jade earrings or other items of jewellery enclosed in a letter were often given to a lover as a pledge of love in the Tang Dynasty.

6　People who were far apart in the old days imagined they could get a big bird or fish to carry letters to their loved ones. Hence the words (魚雁相通) in Chinese mean communication via letters.

JADE POOL

Li Shangyin (813 — 858)

瑤池

李商隱 (813 — 858)

In the Goddess' chamber by the Jade Pool[1],
    wide open the carved windows remain:
The Yellow Bamboo Song[2]
    fills the air with great pain.

With his eight steeds capable of shooting
    thirty thousand miles a day,
Why doesn't Emperor Mu[3] come again?

瑤池阿母綺窗開，
黃竹歌聲動地哀。

八駿日行三萬里，
穆王何事不重來。

---

1 A Goddess in charge of the far-off West who lived beside a pool made of precious jade according to an ancient Chinese legend.

2 A song of mourning written by the Emperor Mu of the Zhou Dynasty (B.C. 1046 — B.C. 256) for his people who died from extremely cold weather.

3 According to the legend, Emperor Mu once paid a visit to the Goddess and was well received. He promised to return in three years but did not survive to keep his promise not withstanding the blessing of the Goddess. The Goddess waited in vain by the open window day after day.

A LETTER TO THE NORTH ON A RAINY NIGHT

Li Shangyin (813 — 858)

夜雨寄北

李商隱 (813 — 858)

You asked the date of my return…
　　　but it's not in sight.
The rain in Bashan[1]
　　　is swelling the autumn pool tonight.

When can we together
　　　trim the candlewicks by the west window,
And share my sentiments
　　　of this Bashan rainy night?

君問歸期未有期，
巴山夜雨漲秋池。

何當共剪西窗燭，
卻話巴山夜雨時。

1　Mountains in eastern Sichuan Province were called Bashan.

Background:
The poet wrote this poem to his wife who was in the north of today's Henan Province (河南省) while he himself was staying in Sichuan Province (四川), hence the title of this poem.

BECAUSE

Li Shangyin (813 — 858)

為有

李商隱（813 — 858）

Behind the mother-of-pearl screen,
    most enchantingly she lay.
Winter was gone in the Phoenix City[1] but
    spring nights filled her with dismay[2].

She chanced to be married
    to a Golden-Tortoise[3] husband;
How ungrateful he was, to leave the sweet
    quilt to attend court before break of day!

為有雲屏無限嬌，
鳳城寒盡怕春宵。

無端嫁得金龜婿，
辜負香衾事早朝。

---

1 Another name for Chang'an, the capital in Tang Dynasty in the old days.

2 The nights in winter are long in northern China. Nights in spring are much shorter (春宵苦短 —
Spring nights are cruelly short as was said) , and this was what annoyed and dismayed her.

3 Court officials of 3rd grade and above had gold-threaded tortoise emblems on their ropes.

AT JIANG VILLAGE

Sikong Shu (720 — 790?)

Back from fishing,
　　my boat I didn't tie.
The moon was setting over Jiang Village –
　　the best time in bed to lie.

Though drifting in the wind overnight,
Still I'm by the shallow water's edge
　　with reed flowers nearby.

江村即事

司空曙 (720 — 790?)

釣罷歸來不繫船，
江村月落正堪眠。

縱然一夜風吹去，
只在蘆花淺水邊。

WRITING ON THE WALL IN THE HOST'S HOUSE

Zhang Wei (around 778)

題長安主人壁

張謂 (約 778 年)

Making friends with people you need gold:
Friendship won't be close
    if little gold you hold.

Despite any promises they may make,
Eventually they're like strangers –
    uncaring and cold.

世人結交須黃金，
黃金不多交不深。

縱令然諾暫相許，
終是悠悠行路心。

Background:
The poet had a short stay in someone's house in Chang'an (today's Xi'an). He was not happy that his host cherished gold (or money) more than friendship. He wrote this poem on the wall before he left.

FAREWELL ON AN ANCIENT MEADOW

Bai Juyi (772 — 846)

賦得古原草送別

白居易 (772 — 846)

Here and there,
　　grasses thrive in the meadow;
Year after year, they wither and grow.

Never can wildfire wipe them out:
Revive they will, when the spring winds blow.

Stretching far and wide,
　　upon an ancient road they intrude;
Glistening and emerald green,
　　into a ruined city they go.

Again I see my dear prince friend off...
Among the lush grasses,
　　parting sentiments overflow.

離離原上草，
一歲一枯榮。

野火燒不盡，
春風吹又生。

遠芳侵古道，
晴翠接荒城，

又送王孫去，
萋萋滿別情。

Background:
Bai Juyi wrote this poem in A.D. 788 at the age of 16. He travelled to Chang'an, the capital, to show it to Gu Kuang (顧況), a very famous poet. Gu was greatly impressed by the talents of the young man especially shown in the second stanza of the poem. He said Bai would have a great career in the capital.

PALACE PLAINT

Bai Juyi (772 — 846)

宮詞

白居易 (772 — 846)

Tears drained and silk handkerchief wetted,
　　but her hope of a dream is gone;
Deep in the night, in the front Palace,
　　beating and singing keep going on.

The Emperor's favour she has lost before
　　getting old...
Leaning on a sandalwood burner,
　　she sits till dawn.

涙盡羅巾夢不成，
夜深前殿按歌聲。

紅顏未老恩先斷，
斜倚熏籠坐到明。

PEACH BLOSSOMS
IN DA LIN TEMPLE

Bai Juyi (772 — 846)

大林寺桃花

白居易（772 — 846）

Gone is nature's fragrance
　　by the fourth month... .
But in the mountain temple,
　　peach trees are just in full bloom.

I always regret
　　spring disappeared without a trace:
Yet here she has come without being known.

人間四月芳菲盡，
山寺桃花始盛開。

長恨春歸無覓處，
不知轉入此中來。

THE VILLAGE AT NIGHT

Bai Juyi (772 — 846)

村夜

白居易 （772 — 846）

Grey, grey is the frosty grass
    where insects chirp songs of woe;
North and south of the village,
    nobody would show.

Stepping outside alone,
    at the wild field I gaze:
In the moonlight,
    buckwheat flowers bright as snow.

霜草蒼蒼蟲切切，
村南村北行人絕。

獨出門前望野田，
月明蕎麥花如雪。

Background:
The poet grew lonesome in a silent autumn night while staying at a village far away from home.

FEELING FOR ONESELF

Bai Juyi (772 — 846)

自感

白居易（772 — 846）

Feasting and travel, sleep and eating
      in time become dull:
For no purpose, one's tied down
      in wine, pipes and strings[1].

Guests are entertained, servants well-fed:
Now I know,

      benefits only to others my office brings.

宴遊寢食漸無味，
杯酒管絃徒繞身。

賓客歡娛僮僕飽，
始知官職為他人。

---

1 Pipes and strings meant music.

A SONG OF THE RIVER AT TWILIGHT

Bai Juyi (772 — 846)

On the water, the setting sun stages a show:
Half of the river is emerald green, half aglow.

What a lovely third night of the ninth month:
Dewdrops look like pearls, the moon a bow.

暮江吟

白居易 (772 — 846)

一道殘陽鋪水中，
半江瑟瑟半江紅。

可憐九月初三夜，
露似真珠月似弓。

HE MANZI

Zhang Hu (around 859)

何滿子

張祜（大約 859 年）

My native land is
　　three thousand miles away;
In the deep Palace,
　　I've been trapped for twenty years.

On hearing the tune of 'He Manzi'[1],

Before you, sir, streaming down are my tears.

故國三千里，
深宮二十年。

一聲何滿子，
雙淚落君前。

1　A famous ancient tragic song written by a Tang Dynasty palace singer called He Manzi.　He committed an offence and submitted this song to the emperor in a plea for mercy.　He failed and was hung.

NIGHT THOUGHTS AT ZHANG TAI

Wei Zhuang (836 — 910)

章臺夜思

韋莊（836 — 910）

A lonesome zither laments in the long night;
In the wind and rain,
    with grief the strings are beset.

Before a solitary lamp,
    the bugles of Chu[1] are heard.
Behind Zhang Tai[2],
    a fading moon has set.

The fragrant grass is about to wither;
But my friend hasn't come yet.

The autumn wild geese
    have turned south again:
Letter from home never would I get.

清瑟怨遙夜，
繞絃風雨哀。

孤燈聞楚角，
殘月下章臺。

芳草已云暮，
故人殊未來。

鄉書不可寄，
秋雁又南回。

---

1 The area around the former Kingdom of Chu in the north. It is now in the southwest of the old city of Chang'an (now the city of Xi'an) in Shaanxi Province. Here the poet indicated that fighting was still going on in the north hence neither could his friend come nor home letters be delivered to him.

2 Name of a place in Chang'an (now the city of Xi'an).

AN IMPRESSION OF JINLING[1]

Wei Zhuang (836 — 910)

金陵圖

韋莊 (836 — 910)

Level are the river sedges, heavy is the rain;
The Six Dynasties[2] are but a dream,
    leaving birds crying in vain.

Most heartless
    are the willows of the old palace,
Like mists,
    veiling the ten-mile bank they remain.

江雨霏霏江草齊，
六朝如夢鳥空啼。

無情最是臺城柳，
依舊煙籠十里堤。

1 Today's Nanjing. It used to be the capital of the Six Dynasties.

2 These were: the East Wu, East Jin, Song, Qi, Liang and Chen Dynasties.

Background:
This poem was written in the spring of A.D. 883 while the poet was touring Nanjing (南京). The beautiful misty scenery of the River-south (江南) evoked his reminiscence of the Six Dynasties which tumbled one after another. This made him worry that the Tang Dynasty, which he knew was very weak at the time, could have a similar fate. His worries were not unfounded. Tang Dynasty eventually collapsed not long thereafter in A.D. 901.

A WARRIOR'S ROBE DISPATCHED TO THE FRONTIER

Chen Yulan[1] (around 8th Century)

寄外征衣

陳玉蘭 (約八世紀)

My husband's guarding the frontier
    and I'm in Wu[2]:
I was worried about him
    when on me the west wind blew.

Countless tears stained every line of my letter:
Has the robe arrived when the cold reached you?

夫戍邊關妾在吳，
西風吹妾妾憂夫。

一行書信千行淚，
寒到君邊衣到無？

---

1 Chen Yulan was the wife of a famous Tang poet, Wang Jia (王駕) who was on official duty in the frontier.
2 Today's Suzhou City in Jiangsu Province.

PALACE PLAINT

Li Jianxun (873 — 952)

宮詞

李建勳 (873 — 952)

Forever shut are the palace doors
    and dancing costumes idly lie.
Grey turn my temples
    yet of the Emperor little know I.

How one envies fallen flowers
    which spring doesn't restrain:
On their way to the outside world,
    the palace ditch they flow by.

宮門常關舞衣閒，
略識君王鬢便斑。

卻羨落花春不管，
御溝流得到人間。

Background:
In those days girls once selected to serve the Emperor were not allowed to leave the palace. They would stay there until old. On the contrary, fallen flowers can freely leave the palace via the palace ditch.

DAWN IN SPRING

Meng Haoran (689 —740)

春曉

孟浩然（689 — 740）

Dawn was missed in a good sleep in spring;
Everywhere I hear birds sing.

Overnight, the wind and rain clamoured;
How many flowers down did they bring?

春眠不覺曉，
處處聞啼鳥。

夜來風雨聲，
花落知多少。

A NIGHT ON TONG LU RIVER REMINISCING ABOUT MY TIME IN GUANGLING

Meng Haoran (689 — 740)

宿桐廬江寄廣陵舊遊

孟浩然（689 — 740）

In the gloomy mountain,
      I listen to the gibbon's howls of woe;
By night, rapidly the cold rivers flow.

On the banks, the wind rustles the leaves ;
Over the solitary sampan,
      the moon casts a glow.

Jiande[1] is not my homeland:
To Wei Yang[2] the memory of my past I owe.

Dispatching to the west-end of the sea afar[3],
Two streams of tears will go.

山暝聽猿愁，
滄江急夜流。

風鳴兩岸葉，
月照一孤舟。

建德非吾土，
維揚憶舊遊。

還將兩行淚，
遙寄海西頭。

---

1 A place on the upstream of the Tong Lu River.

2 The poet's home town, Yangzhou, also known as Wei Yang.

3 Where the city of Yangzhou was situated.

A FAREWELL POEM TO WANG WEI

Meng Haoran (689 — 740)

留別王維

孟浩然（689 — 740）

In loneliness and loneliness,
      for what really do I wait?
Morning after morning,
      I return without my mate.

I wish to live as a hermit,
But to leave an old friend I hate.

Who in power would be helpful?
Under the sun, it's hard to find an intimate.

It's best to put up with loneliness,
And close the old garden gate.

寂寂竟何待，
朝朝空自歸。

欲尋芳草去，
惜與故人違。

當路誰相假，
知音世所稀。

只應守寂寞，
還掩故園扉。

Background:
In the year 730, the poet was in Chang'an as a guest of his good friend, Wang Wei while taking the State Examination. After he learned of his failure, he decided to leave Chang'an for home. Before he went, he left this farewell poem to Wang Wei who was serving as a Court official at the time.

A NIGHT BY THE JIAN DE RIVER

Meng Haoran (689 — 740)

I move my boat
　　to moor by a misty isle.

At nightfall,
　　I fall prey to renewed melancholy.

In the wilderness,
　　the sky has fallen below the trees;

On the clear river,
　　the moon is close to me.

宿建德江

孟浩然（689 — 740）

移舟泊煙渚，
日暮客愁新。

野曠天低樹，
江清月近人。

A VISIT TO YUAN SHI IN VAIN

Meng Haoran (689 — 740)

洛中訪袁
拾遺不遇

孟浩然（689 — 740）

I paid a visit to a man of talent in Luoyang:

He was banished to the south of Jiangling[1].

洛陽訪才子，
江嶺作流人。

I heard plum trees bloom early over there:

They compare not

    with those in a northern spring.

聞説梅花早，
何如北地春。

---

1 Jiangling, also known as Plum Ridge (梅嶺), lies on the south of Da Yu Ling (大庾嶺) in Guangdong. The place is famous for its plum blossoms.

THE GOLD-THREADED GOWN

Du Qiuniang (around 790)

金縷衣

杜秋娘（大約 790 年）

I urge you,
Cherish not the gold-threaded gown;
Cherish instead the days while you're young.

When flowers are in bloom,
　　pick them while you may:
Wait not, lest no flowers
　　but only bare twigs can be found.

勸君莫惜金縷衣！
勸君須惜少年時！

花開堪折直須折，
莫待無花空折枝。

THE BLACK COAT LANE

Liu Yuxi (772 — 842)

烏衣巷

劉禹錫 (772 — 842)

Beside the Red Bird Bridge[1],
    weeds and wild flowers overgrown;
At the entrance of the Black Coat Lane[2],
    the setting sun shone.

Swallows that once nested
    before the halls of Wang and Xie[3],
Into ordinary people's homes had flown.

朱雀橋邊野草花，
烏衣巷口夕陽斜。

舊時王謝堂前燕，
飛入尋常百姓家。

---

1 An ancient floating bridge on the Qinhuai River (秦淮河) in Nanjing.

2 On south bank of the Qinhuai River. Soldiers wearing black coat often passed through this lane which was thus named.

3 Two famous families among the noble and powerful families in the Jin Dynasty in this area that used to be very prosperous. After the noble families left, their houses became deserted and dilapidated. They were later occupied by ordinary families.

THE SHRINE OF THE FOUNDER OF SHU

Liu Yuxi (772 — 842)

蜀 先 主 廟

劉禹錫 (772 — 842)

Great was your heroic spirit
　　between Heaven and Earth:
Thousands of years
　　peoples' reverence for you would span.

You established Shu[1] as one of
　　the three powers[2] like a tripod and
You restored the coinage of Han[3].

With your able minister[4],
　　you founded a new kingdom,
But your son[5] bore
　　no resemblance to a wise man.

Wretched were the former singing-girls of Shu,
To dance before the court of Wei[6] they were sent.

天地英雄氣，
千秋尚凛然。

勢分三足鼎，
業復五銖錢。

得相能開國，
生兒不像賢。

凄涼蜀故伎，
來舞魏宮前。

---

1 The Kingdom of Shu (A.D. 220 — A.D. 263) (蜀國).

2 The Three Kingdoms in the Three Kingdoms Period (A.D. 220 —
　A.D. 280) comprising the Kingdoms of Shu, Wei and Wu.

3 The Han Dynasty (B.C. 206 — A.D. 200).

4 Zhuge Liang (諸葛亮即孔明).

5 Liu Shan (劉禪即阿斗).

6 The Kingdom of Wei (A.D. 220 — A.D. 280). Shu was conquered
　by Wei during the reign of Liu Shan (劉禪即阿斗) in A.D. 263.

Background:
The poet paid tribute to Liu Bei
(劉備) , the founder and first ruler
of the Kingdom of Shu during a
visit to the shrine.

TO BAI JUYI AT OUR FIRST MEETING DURING A DINNER IN YANGZHOU

Liu Yuxi (772 — 842)

Bleak were the mountains of Bar[1]
　　and the waters of Chu[2]:
Wasted were twenty-three years of my life.

Feeling nostalgic,
　　poems I vainly wrote on hearing the flute[3];
Completely worn out,
　　home I barely managed to arrive.

Beside a sunken boat,
　　a thousand sails pass by;
Ahead of a sick trunk,
　　ten thousand trees thrive.

Today a song I've heard you sing –
Wine in hand, I'm for now feeling alive.

巴山楚水淒涼地，
二十三年棄置身。

懷舊空吟聞笛賦，
到鄉翻似爛柯人。

沉舟側畔千帆過，
病樹前頭萬木春。

今日聽君歌一曲，
暫憑杯酒長精神。

1　Mountainous backward region in the east of today's Sichuan Province.

2　The ancient kingdom of Chu (楚國) in the Zhou Dynasty (B.C. 1046 — B.C. 256). It was close to a number of big lakes but very backward and life was difficult. It is in today's Hubei Province.

3　The poet had written many good poems about his nostalgic feelings upon hearing Tartar flutes while he was serving in mountain passes in the frontiers.

A POEM SUBMITTED TO ZHANG JI, BEFORE THE STATE EXAMINATION

Zhu Qingyu (799 — ?)

近試上張籍水部

朱慶餘 (799 — ?)

Last night in the bridal room,
　　　red candles were laid out.
By dawn in the hall,
　　　respect to her parents-in-law she'd pay.

Make-up done,
　　　in a whisper she asks her husband,
"Are my eyebrows painted in a fashionable way?"

洞房昨夜停紅燭，
待曉堂前拜舅姑。

妝罷低聲問夫婿，
畫眉深淺入時無？

Background:
Before the State Examination, the poet submitted this poem to his friend, Zhang Ji (also a poet) who was the Minister of Waterways to seek his opinion as to whether his poem was up to the standard of the examination. The poem was highly regarded by Zhang Ji. The poet passed the examination and was soon recruited by Zhang Ji.

A LETTER TO LI DAN YUAN XI

Wei Yingwu (734 — 792)

Last year, amid flowers we parted;
Today, flowers are blooming –
    another year's gone since we last met.

The vicissitudes of life are unforeseeable;
Sleeping alone, with gloomy
    spring-sorrows I'm beset.

Prone to illness,
    retiring to the countryside is on my mind;
The plight of refugees in my district
    shames me for the pay I get.

Your intended visit is heard:
Over the west chamber,
    many a full moon has risen and set!

寄李儋元錫

韋應物〔734 — 792〕

去年花裏逢君別，
今日花開又一年。

世事茫茫難自料，
春愁黯黯獨成眠。

身多疾病思田里，
邑有流亡愧俸錢。

聞道欲來相問訊，
西樓望月幾回圓。

A LETTER TO MASTER QIU IN AN AUTUMN NIGHT

Wei Yingwu (734 — 792)

秋夜寄丘員外

韋應物（734 — 792）

I miss you on this autumn night,
　　my dear friend;
While strolling, a poem on the cool season
　　I'm about to compose.

Pine cones are falling
　　in the empty mountain;
As a hermit, you probably
　　have not retired to repose.

懷君屬秋夜，
散步詠涼天。

空山松子落，
幽人應未眠。

Background:
Master Qiu was staying in seclusion in a far-off mountain studying Taoism.

THE WEST BROOK IN CHUZHOU

Wei Yingwu (734 — 792)

I particularly love the shadowy grasses
　　the brook-side growing by,
Where golden orioles twitter
　　deep in the trees above high.

Swollen with rain, the spring tide comes
　　rushing in as night falls;
The outback ferry is deserted —
　　a boat swings to and fro nearby.

滁州西澗

韋應物（734 — 792）

獨憐幽草澗邊生，
上有黃鸝深樹鳴。

春潮帶雨晚來急，
野渡無人舟自橫。

TO OFFICIAL YUAN UPON LEAVING THE YANGTZE RIVER

Wei Yingwu (734 — 792)

Sadly, sadly from a beloved friend
    I've just parted;
Drifting, drifting… into the mist I stray.

A Luoyang[1] man is sailing home:
The toll of bells and
    the trees of Guangling[2] are fading away.

Where again shall we meet,
After here we parted today?

Earthly affairs roll like a boat on the waves:
How can the currents be made to stay?

---

1   Luoyang is a city in northern China in the Henan Province which
   is famous for its flowers. Its nickname is Flower City.
2   Guangling is a place in Yang Zhou City in the Jiangsu Province.

初發揚子寄元大
校書

韋應物 (734 — 792)

悽悽去親愛，
泛泛入煙霧。

歸棹洛陽人，
殘鐘廣陵樹。

今朝此為別，
何處還相遇？

世事波上舟，
沿洄安得住？

MEETING AN OLD FRIEND FROM LIANGZHOU ON RIVER HUAI

Wei Yingwu (734 — 792)

淮上喜會
梁州故人

韋應物（734 — 792）

We were once travellers along the River Han.
Often we got drunk when we met before
    saying good-bye.

Like floating clouds, we parted;
Like flowing water, ten years have gone by.

Our hair has become thin and grey;
But our joys and friendship as before lie.

Why don't we return home?
Autumn hills rise above the River Huai.

江漢曾為客，
相逢每醉還。

浮雲一別後，
流水十年間。

歡笑情如舊，
蕭疏鬢已斑。

何因不歸去，
淮上有秋山。

BEES

Luo Yin (833 — 909)

蜂

羅隱（833 — 909）

Whether hilltops or flat land,
All scenic places are under your command.

After honey is made,
    from hundreds of flowers you sipped,
For whom do you toil,
    for whom is this nectar planned?

不論平地與山尖，
無限風光盡被佔。

採得百花成蜜後，
為誰辛苦為誰甜。

WRITTEN FOR CRANE GROVE MONASTERY

Li She (771 — 840?)

題鶴林寺僧舍

李涉 (771 — 840?)

All day long, in a drunken dream I'm;
On hearing spring's ending,
    up the hills I make myself climb.

A monk I chance to talk to
    near a monastery in a bamboos grove:
In this floating life,
    again I've found half-day leisure time.

終日昏昏醉夢間，
忽聞春盡強登山。

因過竹院逢僧話，
又得浮生半日閒。

AT A FEAST IN EASTERN MANOR

Cui Huitong (around 8th century)

How often in a month
　　does the host give a laugh so gay?
At this encounter of ours,
　　do enjoy the wine while we may.

We witness spring's colours
　　pass by like running water:
Flowers withering today bloomed yesterday.

宴城東莊

崔惠童（約八世紀）

一月主人笑幾回？
相逢相值且銜杯。

眼看春色如流水，
今日殘花昨日開。

RIVER SOUTH SONG

Li Yi (748 — 829)

江南曲

李益 (748 — 829)

Married to a Qu Tang[1] merchant:
Morning after morning,
    our reunion is denied.

Had I known the tide is faithful,
I'd have married someone
    who plays with the tide.

嫁得瞿塘賈，
朝朝誤妾期。

早知潮有訊，
嫁與弄潮兒。

1   A place near the Three Gorges along the Yangtze River.

ASCENDING THE CITY WALLS WHERE SURRENDER WAS ACCEPTED

Li Yi (748 — 829)

夜上受降城聞笛聲

李益 (748 — 829)

Beneath the Hui Le Peak[1],
　　the sands look like snow;
Beyond the surrender-accepting walls,
　　the moonlight resembles rime.

From nowhere comes
　　the tunes on a reed flute,
Throughout the night,
　　for their homes all soldiers pine.

回樂峰前沙似雪，
受降城外月如霜。

不知何處吹蘆管，
一夜征人盡望鄉。

1　A peak of a mountain situated in southwest Lingwu in Ningxia Province (寧夏省).

EXPEDITION TO THE NORTH

Li Yi (748 — 829)

從軍北征

李益（748 — 829）

After a snowfall in Heaven Mount[1],
    the wind[2] is freezing cold;
All over the place, the flutes
    are playing 'Hardships on the Road'.

In the desert, thirty thousand soldiers
    instantly turn their heads —
A distant sight of homeland
    in the moonlight all behold.

天山雪後海風寒，
橫笛吹遍行路難。

磧裏征人三十萬，
一時回首月中看。

---

1 Tian Shan (天山) . One of the largest mountains in northwestern China.
2 Referred to desert wind. The sea was thousands of miles away.

SEEING OFF MASTER WEN

Zhu Fang (? — 788)

As you travel to the world's end far, far away,
Floating clouds and running water
      are naturally with you all the way.

Throughout our lives we're like passers-by,
Why call this a parting at all today?

送溫臺

朱放 (? — 788)

渺渺天涯君去時，
浮雲流水自相隨。

人生一世長如客，
何必今朝是別離。

AT THE FRONTIER (1)

Wang Changling (698 — 757)

We watered our horses
  while crossing the autumn river:
Freezing was the water,
  the wind cut like a blade.

Over the level sands
  the sun hadn't quite set;
In the gathering gloom,
  the view of Lin Tao[1] began to fade.

In the Battle of the Great Wall[2] of yore,
High was the fighting spirit displayed.

As ever, yellow dust continues its reign;
Weeds and thistles white bones invade.

---

1   A place in Gansu near the border. It is the starting point of the ancient Great Wall.

塞下曲 （1）

王昌齡（698 — 757）

飲馬渡秋水，
水寒風似刀。

平沙日未沒，
黯黯見臨洮。

昔日長城戰，
咸言意氣高。

黃塵足今古，
白骨亂蓬蒿。

2 This was a bitter war between the Hans and the invading Turfans which took place in A.D. 714. Tens of
thousands were killed. It was recorded that the flow of the nearby Tao River was once disrupted by the large
number of dead bodies.

AT THE FRONTIER (2)

Wang Changling (698 — 757)

Cicadas chirp in the empty mulberry grove
Along the autumn Xiao Pass[1] road.

In and out of the frontier we travel:
Everywhere the reeds have turned gold.

Warriors from You and Bing[2]
Forever tarry in battlefields till old.

Imitate not the roving heroes,
Who brag their chestnut steeds are bold.

1 One of the four ancient passes in the present Ningxia County in
  Gansu Province. It was autumn in the northern frontier in the 8th
  month on the lunar calendar.

2 Ancient names of far north places in today's Hebei and Shaanxi
  Provinces.

Background:
The poet reminded people not to be preoccupied with their success
in the frontier and not to forget about returning home.

塞下曲（2）

王昌齡（698 — 757）

蟬鳴空桑林，
八月蕭關道。

出塞復入塞，
處處黃蘆草。

從來幽並客，
皆向沙場老。

莫學遊俠兒，
矜誇紫騮好。

BEYOND THE FRONTIER

Wang Changling (698 — 757)

It's the same bright moon as in Qin[1]
  and the same boundary pass as in Han[2],
From the myriad-mile expeditions,
  return not a single man.

If the Flying General
  of Dragon City[3] were here,
Never would the Tartar horsemen
  be allowed to cross Yin Shan[4].

出塞

王昌齡 （698 — 757）

秦時明月漢時關，
萬里長征人未還。

但使龍城飛將在，
不教胡馬度陰山。

1 & 2 Two different Dynasties signifying the long span of time during which warriors were stationed outside to stop raids from the northern barbarians, the Tartars (or the Xiong Nu).

3 General Li Guang (飛將軍李廣) (died in B.C. 119), a famous general in Han Dynasty who repeatedly defeated the Tartars (or Xiong Nu tribesmen) and was much dreaded by them.

4 A mountain in northern Inner Mongolia.

A WIFE'S LAMENT

Wang Changling (698 — 757)

A young lady knows not
    sorrows in her bower:
In bright finery on a spring day,
    she ascends an ornate tower.

Suddenly the colour of
    roadside willows catches her eyes:
She regrets urging her husband
    to seek honours and power.

閨怨

王昌齡（698 — 757）

閨中少婦不知愁，
春日凝妝上翠樓。

忽見陌頭楊柳色，
悔教夫婿覓封侯。

Background:
Her husband volunteered to
fight a battle at the frontier and
she was left alone at home.

FAREWELL TO XIN JIAN AT HIBISCUS TOWER

Wang Changling (698 — 757)

芙蓉樓送辛漸

王昌齡 (698 — 757)

In freezing rain mingled with the river,
    by night I came to Wu[1].
At dawn I see you off,
    lonely as the mountains of Chu[2].

Tell them my heart is
    as pure as ice in a jade pot,
If relatives and friends in Luoyang ask you.

寒雨連江夜入吳，
平明送客楚山孤。

洛陽親友如相問，
一片冰心在玉壺。

---

1   The former domain of the ancient Kingdom of Wu (吳國) in the Zhou Dynasty (B.C. 1046 — B.C. 256) around today's Jiangsu Province.

2   The former domain of the ancient Kingdom of Chu (楚國) in the Zhou Dynasty (B.C. 1046 — B.C. 256) around today's Hunan and Hubei Provinces. Xin Jian, a friend of the poet, was leaving Wu for Luoyang via Chu.

A SOLDIER'S SONG (1)

Wang Changling (698 — 757)

從軍行 （Ⅰ）

王昌齡 (698 — 757)

Before the Pipa[1], soldiers dance to a new tune;
As ever, with yearning for home
　　　　the mountain pass is strewn.

Perplexing sorrows at the border
　　　　are endless to hear;
Shining on the Great Wall
　　　　is the high-hanging autumn moon.

琵琶起舞換新聲，
總是關山舊別情。

撩亂邊愁聽不盡，
高高秋月照長城。

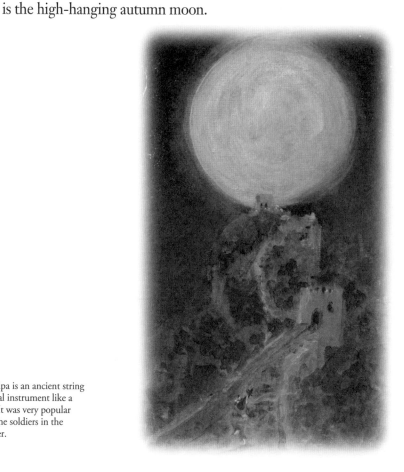

1 The Pipa is an ancient string
　musical instrument like a
　lute. It was very popular
　with the soldiers in the
　frontier.

A SOLDIER'S SONG (2)

Wang Changling (698 — 757)

West of the beacon fire wall
    stands a hundred-foot tower.
Alone I sit in the autumn sea breeze[1]
    during the dusk hour.

Being played on the Tartar flute is
    "The Moon in the Mountain Pass":
Ten thousand miles away,
    she's spiritless and sad in her ornate bower.

從軍行 （2）

王昌齡 (698 — 757)

烽火城西百尺樓，
黃昏獨坐海風秋。

更吹羌笛關山月，
無那金閨萬里愁。

---

1   Breeze that blew from the Green Sea (青海) or West Sea (西海) which is now called Qinghai Lake (青
海湖). The poet was attached to the expedition army stationed in the northwest frontier near the Lake.

AT THE SOUTH FERRY OF LIZHOU

Wen Tingyun (812 — 870)

利州南渡

温庭筠 (812 — 870)

Placidly the empty waters
  face the slanting sunray;
Blending with the green mountain mist,
  the crooked islands look vast and vague.

By the willow,
  people rest, waiting for the ferry's return;
On the waves,
  a boat is seen leaving as horses neigh;

Over several thickets of sand-grass,
  a flock of gulls scatters;
Across the boundless riverside fields,
  a single egret wings its way.

Who'd understand why
  I'm rowing in search of Fan Li¹?
On the misty waters of the Five Lakes²,
  from worldly affairs he alone stayed away.

澹然空水對斜暉，
曲島蒼茫接翠微。

波上馬嘶看棹去，
柳邊人歇待船歸。

數叢沙草群鷗散，
萬頃江田一鷺飛。

誰解乘舟尋范蠡，
五湖煙水獨忘機。

---

1 Fan Li (范蠡 B.C. 536 — B.C. 448) was a minister of the Kingdom of Yue (越國). He succeeded in assisting the King of Yue (越王勾踐 B.C. 496 — B.C. 464) to defeat the Wu Kingdom (吳國). Legend has it that upon success, he resigned from court and went sailing freely and happily on the Five Lakes with Xi Shi (西施), the beautiful concubine of the King of Yue. He later became a very rich and respected merchant and a great philanthropist.

2 Tai Lake (太湖) and the four adjacent small lakes.

A YOUNG PLANTAIN LEAF BEFORE UNFOLDING

Qian Yu (8ᵗʰ Century)

未展芭蕉

錢珝 (八世紀)

A cold smokeless candle, green and dry[1];
Like a maiden's heart
    hidden in the spring chill, timid and shy.

What message is concealed inside the roll[1]?
It can't escape the east wind's prying eye.

冷燭無煙綠蠟乾，
芳心猶捲怯春寒。

一緘書札藏何事，
會被東風暗拆看。

---

1 Before unfolding, a young plantain leaf resembles a candle or a roll.

Background:
This is a metaphor.   A young plantain leaf waits for the east wind (i.e. spring) to unfold it. This is likened to a maiden who waits for love to unfold her heart.

YEARNING UNDER THE MOON

Zhang Jiuling (673 — 740)

The bright moon emerges from the sea;
At opposite ends of the earth,
  this moment we share.

Lovers complain this endless night:
All night long, love emotions flare.

The moonlight all over is lovely
  as I put out the candle;
The damp of the dew is felt so a coat I wear.

A handful of moonlight to you I can't offer;
Retire I would, to dream of our sweet affair.

望月懷遠

張九齡 (673 — 740)

海上生明月，
天涯共此時。

情人怨遙夜，
竟夕起相思。

滅燭憐光滿，
披衣覺露滋。

不堪盈手贈，
還寢夢佳期。

EVER SINCE YOU LEFT

Zhang Jiuling (673 — 740)

Ever since you left, my dear,
I no longer tend
    the unfinished weaving on the loom.

Pining for you,
    I lose my radiance night after night,
Just like the ever-waning full moon.

自君之出矣

張九齡 (673 — 740)

自君之出矣，
不復理殘機。

思君如滿月，
夜夜減清輝。

REFLECTIONS (1)

Zhang Jiuling (678 — 740)

A lone wild goose comes from the sea –
A pond below it daren't see.

With a side glance,
　　it notices a pair of kingfishers[1]
Nesting in a Three-pearl tree[2].

High atop a precious tree and
　　exposed to golden shots[3],
Are they fear-free?

Fine clothing invites finger-pointing;
High ranking provokes the gods' jealousy.

Now I roam far and high –
How can hunters prey on me?

感遇 (1)

張九齡 (678 — 740)

孤鴻海上來，
池潢不敢顧。
側見雙翠鳥，
巢在三珠樹。

矯矯珍木巔，
得無金丸懼。
美服患人指，
高明逼神惡。

今我遊冥冥，
戈者何所慕？

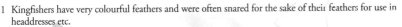

1　Kingfishers have very colourful feathers and were often snared for the sake of their feathers for use in
　headdresses etc.

2　A precious tree with pearls on its leaves mentioned in an ancient fairy book called *the Book of Mountains
　and Seas* (《山海經》).

3　Small metal balls thrown from a sling by hunters in ancient times.

Background:
The poet was an upright and outspoken Deputy Prime Minister (右丞相) in Tang Dynasty in A.D. 736.
He hinted that people with fine clothing and in high positions were in danger of being slandered by their
opponents.　He himself was slandered by an opponent, Li Linfu (李林甫) and banished in A.D. 738.
This poem reflected his bitter experience.

REFLECTIONS (2)

Zhang Jiuling (678 — 740)

感遇 (2)

張九齡 (678 — 740)

Red oranges grow in River South; Through all winter, green the trees stay.	江南有丹橘， 經冬猶綠林。
It isn't due to the warm soil: A will to endure the wintry cold they display.	豈伊地氣暖， 自有歲寒心。
They're fit for 　　　presenting to the honoured guests – Yet immense obstacles stand in the way.	可以薦嘉客， 奈何阻重深。
One's fate is what one encounters: It comes in cycles – seek it none may.	運命惟所遇， 循環不可尋。
People talk only of 　　　planting peaches and plums, Don't orange trees shelter us from the sunray?	徒言樹桃李， 此木豈無陰？

Background:

The poet was one of the very few southerners who rose to the top rank in the Imperial Court. Soon after his banishment, the poet returned to his home in Qu Jiang (曲江) in Guangdong Province in southern China. He hinted in this poem that he accepted his fate but foretold that in time the same fate would befall his opponent. He argued that fruit trees in the south (alluding to southerners) were as good as those in the north (alluding to northerners).

SPRING WALK

Li Hua (715 — 766)

Under the city walls of Yi Yang,
    thick the grass grows;
Eastward and westward the stream flows.

Vainly, birds sing
    along the road in the spring hill;
Unnoticed, flowers
    fall from fragrant trees as no one's close.

春行即興

李華〔715 — 766〕

宜陽城下草萋萋，
澗水東流復向西。

芳樹無人花自落，
春山一路鳥空啼。

AUTUMN AT TONG GUAN COURIER POST ON MY WAY TO THE CAPITAL

Xu Hun (around 844)

秋日赴闕題潼
驛樓

許渾（大約 844 年）

Red leaves rustle in the evening wind;
With a gourd of wine, the long pavilion[1] I'm in.

To Tai Hua Mountain[2]
　　the fading clouds return;
Over Zhong Tiao Hill[3]
　　the light rain sets in.

The colours of trees
　　revolve around the Pass;
The sound of the river
　　entering the distant sea becomes thin.

The Imperial City[4] we'll reach tomorrow;
But I still dream of rivers and hills
　　and the life therein.

紅葉晚蕭蕭，
長亭酒一瓢。

殘雲歸太華，
疏雨過中條。

樹色隨關迥，
河聲入海遙。

帝鄉明日到，
猶自夢漁樵。

1　A place for travellers to rest.
　　The poet stayed overnight at an
　　inn beside the long pavilion at
　　a courier station in Tong Guan
　　where he enjoyed his wine and
　　wrote this poem before re-
　　boarding his boat for Chang'an
　　to take up a new post.

2　Hua Shan (華山), in the
　　southwest of Tong Guan
　　County, Shaanxi Province.

3　Zhong Tiao Shan (中條山),
　　in the southeast of Yongji
　　county, Shanxi Province.

4　Chang'an, the capital.

AUTUMN THOUGHTS

Xu Hun (around 844)

秋思

許渾 (大約 844 年)

Qi trees sigh in the west wind
　　bringing autumn to my pillow and bed.
Oh, how I miss the time in the Chu[1] mountains
　　and Xiang[2] waters that we had!

Aloud we sang but now
　　I'd cover up the mirror:
Alas, a youngster of yesterday
　　has got a white-haired head!

琪樹西風枕簟秋，
楚雲湘水憶同遊。

高歌一曲掩明鏡，
昨日少年今白頭。

1&2　Places around today's Hubei and Hunan Provinces respectively.

AN EVENING VIEW ON THE WEST CITY TOWER IN XIAN YANG [1]

Xu Hun (around 844)

Once on the tall city walls,
    in sight is an immensity of sorrow…
Reminding me of Tingzhou [2]
    are the sedges and willow.

The clouds rise above the stream
    as the sun sinks below the attic;
The mountain rain's imminent
    as all over the tower, winds blow.

Birds descend on green weeds
    as night falls in the Royal Garden of Qin [3];
Cicadas would chirp in the Palace of Han [4]
    by autumn when yellow the leaves grow.

One mustn't ask about the past:
Coming from home in the east,
    the Wei River [5] continues to flow.

咸陽城西樓晚眺

許渾（大約 844 年）

一上高城萬里愁，
蒹葭楊柳似汀洲。

溪雲初起日沉閣，
山雨欲來風滿樓。

鳥下綠蕪秦苑夕，
蟬鳴黃葉漢宮秋。

行人莫問當年事，
故國東來渭水流。

1 Later known as Chang'an, the capital in Tang Dynasty.

2 Old name of a county in Fujian Province where the poet once served. It is now called Chang Ting County.

3&4 These referred to the Qin Dynasty (B.C. 221 — B.C. 206) and the Han Dynasty (B.C. 206 — A.D. 220). Xian Yang was the capital of both these Dynasties.

5 A river running eastwards from Gansu Province passing by Xian Yang before joining the Yellow River in Zhengzhou in Henan Province .

Background:
The poet was homesick while serving in Xian Yang, some 600 miles from his home in Jiangsu Province.

FOR SOMEONE

Zhang Bi (around 930)

Since we parted, to the Xie's home
    longingly I dreamed I went:
The small corridor was winding,
    the railing bent.

Only the spring moon
    in the courtyard is full of love:
It still lights up fallen flowers
    for a separated gent.

寄人

張泌 (大約 930 年)

別夢依依到謝家，
小廊迴合曲闌斜。

多情只有春庭月，
猶為離人照落花。

THE COLD FOOD FESTIVAL [1]

Han Hong (year of birth and death unknown)

寒食

韓翃 〔生卒年不詳〕

Nowhere in the springtime city
    would petals not fly and spin;
During the Cold Food Festival,
    imperial willows bend before the east wind.

At dusk in the Han Palace,
    candles are lit and passed [2]:
Their light smoke drifts into the homes
    of the Five Dukes [3] and their kin.

春城無處不飛花，
寒食東風御柳斜。

日暮漢宮傳蠟燭，
輕煙散入五侯家。

1 A historic festival starting 105 days after the winter solstice (i.e. 2 days before Qing Ming festival) in
  commemoration of the tragic death of Jie Zhitui (介之推) , a famed scholar and statesman of the Jin
  Dynasty (A.D. 265 — A.D. 420).
  In the later part of his life, Jie had lost interest in politics and retired to the mountains. He did not
  respond to calls on him by the Emperor to come out to serve the court again. The Emperor ordered fire
  to be set to the mountain to force him out. Jie did not come out and was burnt to death. The nation
  mourned and the Emperor greatly regretted his action and ordered, on the anniversary of his death,
  that no fire should be lit and only cold food should be eaten. Henceforth, fires were banned for three
  consecutive days during this time every year.

2 This is a veiled criticism of the royal Tang family. The poet hinted that people in the palace and the
  royal families did not observe the ban. He used the word Han (漢) instead of Tang (唐) to avoid direct
  accusation which might attract punishment.

3 The Five Dukes were the five uncles of the Han Emperor, namely Wang Tan, Wang Shang, Wang Li,
  Wang Gen and Wang Feng (王譚、王商、王立、王根及王逢).

TESTAMENT TO MY GRAND NEPHEW XIANG UPON REACHING LAN PASS IN EXILE

Han Yu (768 — 824)

I submitted a petition in the morn to the Ninth Sky[1],
And was banished at eve
  eight thousand li's to Chaozhou[2] thereby.

Intent on removing
  a bad policy for the Emperor[3],
I spared not my frail and
  declining years to give it a try.

Clouds pile up across Qin Ridge[4] –
  but where's my home?
Snow blocks Lan Pass at which the horses shy.

Coming all the way from afar,
  your intention I know:
To gather my bones –
  beside the unwholesome river[5] they'd lie.

左遷至藍關示姪孫湘

韓愈 (768 — 824)

一封朝奏九重天，
夕貶潮州路八千。

欲為聖明除弊事，
肯將衰朽惜殘年。

雲橫秦嶺家何在，
雪擁藍關馬不前。

知汝遠來應有意，
好收吾骨瘴江邊。

1　An unofficial name of the imperial court. Known as such because one had to pass through nine big gates to get to the court.

2　A city in Guangdong Province in the far south which was eight thousand li's (or some three thousand miles) away from the capital.

3　In A.D. 819, a nation-wide celebration of the arrival of relics of the Buddha (佛骨) was being organized to please the Emperor. As a vice-minister, the poet petitioned against such activities condemning these as wasteful which would not bring longevity to the Emperor but would add to the sufferings of the people. His petition greatly upset the Emperor who intended to have him hanged but eventually decreed his immediate exile.

4　A big mountain ridge in the south of Shaanxi Province separating southern and northern China.

5　Northerners used to believe mountains and rivers in the south were full of harmful vapours (瘴氣) giving rise to fatal diseases such as malaria. Han feared he would die in the south but he survived and was recalled to the capital in A.D. 821 and promoted. He died in A.D. 824, aged 56.

CROSSING THE HAN RIVER

Li Pin (9ᵗʰ century)

渡漢江

李頻（九世紀）

Beyond the Mountain[1],
  letters from home were cut off;
Having passed through winter,
  spring is again here.

More timid I grow
  when getting close to home:
I daren't ask the person coming near.

嶺外音書絕，
經冬復立春。

近鄉情更怯，
不敢問來人。

---

1 This is Da Yu Ling（大庾嶺）which separates Guangdong from the mid-China provinces. The poet was posted to south of Da Yu Ling, far away from his home with which he had lost contact for two years.

FAREWELL TO LING CHE

Liu Changqing (early 8th century)

Green, green is the monastery
    in the bamboo grove;
Faint, faint the toll of evening bell far away.

In a bamboo cap
    carrying the slanting sunlight,
Deep into the blue mountain,
    home alone you make your way.

送靈澈

劉長卿 (八世紀初)

蒼蒼竹林寺，
杳杳鐘聲晚。

荷笠帶斜陽，
青山獨歸遠。

PALACE PLAINT IN SPRING

Du Xunhe (846 — 904)

春宮怨

杜荀鶴 (846 — 904)

Beauty and elegance
　　have long proved a snare;
Before the mirror,
　　too weary am I to dress up fair.

If a pretty face wins not
　　the Emperor's favour,
What adornments should I wear?

Birds chirp in the warm breeze;
Flower shadows overlap
　　in the midday sun's glare.

Year after year,
　　with girls from the streams of Yue[1],
Sweet memories of hibiscus plucking I share.

早被嬋娟誤，
欲妝臨鏡慵。

承恩不在貌，
教妾若為容。

風暖鳥聲碎，
日高花影重。

年年越溪女，
相憶採芙蓉。

---

1 The Kingdom of Yue (越國 ？— B.C. 222).

Background:
Xi Shi (西施) , a very beautiful girl in ancient China, was one of the clothes-washing girls by the streams of Yue before becoming the favorite concubine of the King of Yue's because of her beauty. The girl depicted in this poem was one of those clothes-washing girls. Though equally beautiful, her fate was entirely different from that of Xi Shi. Some scholars suggested that the poet was indirectly alluding to himself not winning the favour of the Tang Emperor notwithstanding that he was equally talented as his peers in the Imperial Court.

THE SONG OF GE SHU

Xi Biren (year of birth and death unknown)

哥舒歌

西鄙人（生卒年不詳）

The Plough hangs at great height;
Ge Shu[1] carries a sabre in the night.

Cross Lin Tao[2] the Tartars dare not,
Though they still pry our horse-raising site.

北斗七星高，
哥舒夜帶刀。

至今窺牧馬，
不敢過臨洮。

1　Ge Shu was a famous army commander in the frontier. He repeatedly defected and drove away the Tartar invaders who were all scared to hear his name.

2　A place in present day Gansu Province on the western frontier bordering Tibet.

SONG OF LIANGZHOU[1]

Wang Han (around 710)

涼州曲

王翰 (大約 710 年)

Fine grape wine
    in luminous cups of jade[2]:
To drink I want but the summoning Pipa[3]
    on horseback is played.

Laugh not, my dear friend,
    if I lie drunk on the battlefield:
How many ever returned from battles anyway?

葡萄美酒夜光杯，
欲飲琵琶馬上催。

醉臥沙場君莫笑，
古來征戰幾人回。

---

1 A place in the northwestern frontier, now inside Gansu Province.

2 The ancient luminous cups were made of jade with very thin wall such that it looked translucent when filled with grape wine.

3 A pipa is an ancient string musical instrument like a lute. The troop was about to set off when it was played.

ON LEAVING JADE PASS AFTER MY BROTHER AND I BOTH FAILED IN THE STATE EXAMINATION

Lu Lun (742 — 798)

與從弟瑾同下第
出關言別

盧綸 (742 — 798)

Gone are the flowers, shadowy is the willow;
Twisty and unending is the official road
      where gloomy the grasses grow[1].

Before the wine,
      we've become thousand-mile travellers:
Over the mountain,
      our home-yearning thoughts vainly flow.

雜花飛盡柳陰陰，
官路逶迤綠草深。

對酒已成千里客，
望山空寄兩鄉心。

---

1 The poet, having failed in the State Examination, was reluctant to return home. He left his brother and went out of the Jade Pass to seek an employment. He knew his road to the imperial court (i.e. getting an appointment in court) was tortuous.

AT THE FRONTIER (1)

Lu Lun (742 — 798)

塞下曲 （1）

盧綸 (742 — 798)

The moon was blotted out;
    the wild geese flew at great height.
Chan Yue[1] was sneaking away in the night.

Our light cavalry
    was about to give a chase;
The heavy snow
    covered bows and swords outright.

月黑雁飛高，
單于夜遁逃。

欲將輕騎逐，
大雪滿弓刀。

1 The chief of the Tartar army who was defeated.

AT THE FRONTIER (2)

Lu Lun (742 — 798)

In the gloomy forest,
    a scary gust of wind blew;
In the night, his bow the General drew.

By dawn searching for the arrow,
They find a rock it had struck through.

塞下曲 （2）

盧綸（742 — 798）

林草暗驚風，
將軍夜引弓。

平明尋白羽，
沒在石稜中。

Background:
It was believed that the poet was trying to convince others that the army was very strong as evidenced by the exceptional power of the General's arrow.

FAREWELL TO DEPUTY PREFECTS — LI DEGRADED TO WU GORGE[1], WANG DEGRADED TO CHANGSHA[2]

Gao Shi (700 — 765)

送李少府貶峽中
王少府貶長沙

高適 (700 — 765)

Alas my friends, at this parting how do you feel?
Stay your horses, enjoy your wine –
    I'd ask about the places you're assigned.

Amid the howls of Wu Gorge gibbons,
    your tears would roll;
From the returning Hengyang wild geese,
    your messages I'd find[3].

Afar you'd travel in an autumn sail
    along the Green Maple River[4];
With scattered ancient trees,
    the Baidi Town[5] is lined.

Today, the court of wisdom often grants favour[6]:
Let not a temporary separation unsettle your mind.

嗟君此別意何如？
駐馬銜杯問謫居。

巫峽啼猿數行淚，
衡陽歸雁幾封書。

青楓江上秋帆遠，
白帝城邊古木疏。

聖代即今多雨露，
暫時分手莫躊躇。

---

1 One of the Three Gorges on the Yangtze River in Sichuan Province. Prefect Li was banished to this area.

2 The capital city of Hunan Province.

3 Prefect Wang was banished to Han Yang County in Hunan Province. In ancient times, people in the faraway south sometimes bound messages to the legs of wild geese that were flying north hoping that they could carry them to the recipients.

4 A river in Chang Sha in Hunan Province.

5 An historic town along the Three Gorges in Sichuan Province.

6 Pardon granted by the Emperor.

FAREWELL TO DONG DA

Gao Shi (700 — 765)

For a thousand miles, clouds are
    tinted yellow in the setting sun's glow;
The northern wind
    buffets the wild geese in the heavy snow.

Don't worry about not meeting
    an intimate on your way:
Of you, who in the whole world doesn't know?

別董大

高適 (700 — 765)

千里黃雲白日曛，
北風吹雁雪紛紛。

莫愁前路無知己，
天下誰人不識君。

LISTENING TO THE FLUTE IN THE MOUNTAIN PASS

Gao Shi (700 — 765)

塞上聽吹笛

高適 (700 — 765)

Snow has retreated from the barbarian sky,
    horses returned to their raising site;
The Tartar flute resounds
    in the barracks in bright moonlight.

May I ask where the plum blossoms are falling[1]?
They're blown all over the mountain pass
    throughout the night.

雪淨胡天牧馬還，
月明羌笛戍樓間。

借問梅花何處落，
風吹一夜滿關山。

---

1 'Plum Blossoms are Falling' (梅花落) was a popular ancient tune in mid-China from where the poet came. Plum trees do not grow in the frontier area in the far north. The poet was homesick upon hearing the tune which aroused his imagination.

UNTITLED

Anonymous

雜詩

無名氏

Grasses grow thick in the rain
　　as the Cold Food Festival[1] nears;
Willows are reflected along the bank
　　as young wheat with the wind veers.

We both have our homes
　　but we cannot go back:
Oh, cuckoo, cry not in my ears[2]!

近寒食雨草萋萋，
著麥苗風柳映堤。

等是有家歸未得，
杜鵑休向耳邊啼。

1　A historic festival starting
　　105 days after the winter
　　solstice (i.e 2 days before
　　Qing Ming Festival) in
　　commemoration of the
　　tragic death of Jie Zhitui, a
　　famed scholar and statesman
　　of the Jin Dynasty (晉朝
　　B.C. 265 — B.C. 420).

2　The call of a cuckoo is a
　　distinct four note sound
　　similar to "why not go
　　home" in Chinese (不如歸
　　去). The poet was pining
　　for his home but could not
　　go back. He therefore hated
　　to hear its call.

THE JADE FOUNTAIN STREAM

Lady Xiang Yi (year of birth and death unknown)

Drunk are the red trees
　　　amid autumn hues;
By night I play my strings
　　　beside the emerald stream.

Reunion is beyond reach:
In the wind and rain,
　　　remote and obscure it'd seem.

題玉泉溪

湘驛女子（生卒年不詳）

紅樹醉秋色，
碧溪彈夜絃。

佳期不可再，
風雨杳如年。

THE TEMPLE OF QU YUAN [1]

Dai Shulun (732 — 789)

Endlessly the Yuan[2] and Xiang[3] flow;
Qu Yuan's resentments run so deep.

Autumn wind rises as night falls;
Maples in the grove weep.

三閭廟

戴叔倫 (732 — 789)

湘沅流不盡，
屈子怨何深。

日暮秋風起，
蕭蕭楓樹林。

---

1 Qu Yuan (屈原) was a great patriotic scholar and poet of the Kingdom of Chu (楚國) in the Warring Period (B.C. 221 — B.C. 189). His political views were not accepted by the Court of Chu. He hence lived in exile in the River South in despair. On the 5th day of the 5th month of the lunar calendar, he killed himself by jumping into a river. He was remembered on this day for his patriotism and achievement in literature through the centuries. This day is called the Dragon Boat Festival (端午節) .

2&3 The Yuan River runs from Guizhou into Hunan Province and the Xiang River from Guangxi into Hunan Province. These two rivers were often mentioned in Qu's writings. Here the poet symbolized the endless nature of Qu's resentment.

AT THE FRONTIER

Dai Shulun (732 — 789)

塞上曲

戴叔倫 (732 — 789)

Flying all over Mount Yin[1] are flags of Han[2]:
Not a single Tartar[3] horseman
      is allowed to return to their clan.

My life I've devoted to my country:
What's the need to enter Jade Pass[4] a living man?

漢家旌旗滿陰山，
不遣胡兒匹馬還。

願得此生長報國，
何須生入玉門關。

1 A large mountain in Inner Mongolia, northern China.

2 Chinese.

3 Barbarians on the northern Chinese border.

4 A major ancient pass in northwest border in Gansu Province near Dunhuang (敦煌) through which soldiers returned to their homeland.

FAREWELL ON A MOUNTAIN RIDGE

Quan Deyu (year of birth and death unknown)

嶺上逢久別者
又別

權德輿 (生卒年不詳)

Ten years ago we parted;
On this expedition route again we met.

"Where's your horse heading for?"
"Towards the countless mounts in the sunset."

十年曾一別，
征路此相逢。

馬首向何處，
夕陽千萬峯。

AT CITY SOUTH MANOR

Cui Hu (around 790)

題都城南莊

崔護〔大約 790 年〕

This day last year inside these gates,
Red and shining on each other
    were the peach blossoms and your face.

Now the peach blossoms
    remain smiling in the spring breeze,
But you're gone without a trace.

去年今日此門中，
人面桃花相映紅。

人面不知何處去，
桃花依舊笑春風。

A WATER TUNE

Anonymous (8th century)

Below the boundless desert,

    the sun sets in the great wild west;

High and low, stars twinkle

    above the mountain[1] crest.

Beacon fires flare atop several isolated hills:

Warriors throughout the camp

    await battle drumbeats with zest.

水調歌

無名氏（八世紀）

平沙落日大荒西，
隴上明星高復低。

孤山幾處看烽火，
壯士連營候鼓鼙。

---

1 Long Mountain (隴山) in today's Gansu Province. It was frontier in Tang Dynasty where battles after battles were fought against the invading Tartars.

A CICADA OUTSIDE THE PRISON

Luo Binwang (619 — ?)

在獄詠蟬

駱賓王（619 — ?）

An autumn cicada chirps;
A prisoner in southern cap[1] ponders deep.

西陸蟬聲唱，
南冠客思深。

Hardly can one bear its dark hairy shadow;
Before a whitehead, it has come to weep.

不堪玄鬢影，
來對白頭吟。

Under heavy dew its flight is clogged;
In strong wind a sharp voice is hard to keep.

露重飛難進，
風多響易沉。

A noble character nobody believes:
Who would speak for me? Who indeed?

無人信高潔，
誰為表余心。

---

1 The poet was a court official in A.D. 678. Empress Wu Zetian (武則天) was displeased with the criticism contained in his submissions and had him imprisoned. Later in A.D. 684, he was involved in a rebellion against Empress Wu. He refused to take off his southern headgear as a gesture of protest.

IN THE YEAR A.D. 879[1]

Cao Song (A.D. ? — 902)

The swamp region
    has fallen into a fighting zone:
How can the people
    enjoy a peaceful life of their own?

Talk not, my friend,
    of award of honours and nobility:
A general's victory is built
    upon ten thousand rotting bones!

己亥歲

曹松 (? — 902)

澤國江山入戰圖，
生民何計樂樵蘇？

憑君莫話封侯事，
一將功成萬骨枯。

---

1 The time (A.D. 879) was close to the end of the Tang Dynasty when widespread fighting took place incessantly causing great sufferings to the people.

APPENDIX
附錄

Two Song Poems and Six Tang and Song Lyrics
宋詩兩首及唐宋詞六首

APPENDIX

Two Song Poems and Six Tang & Song Lyrics

The purpose of this Appendix is to arouse readers' interest in the equally beautiful Song poems (宋 詩) and the fascinating Tang and Song lyrics (唐宋詞) after they have read the above 202 Tang poems.

The two Song poems included here were written by Lu You (陸游), a well-known patriotic poet who advocated waging of full-scale war to re-capture the north provinces from the Jurchen invader (金人) but without success. With a legacy of over 9,400 poems, he is the most prolific poet in ancient China. The first one recorded his reminiscences of the encounter with his wife whilst the second one was his last poem written at his dying bed at the age of 85.

Tang and Song lyrics originated in the middle to late Tang Dynasty. They took a different and more enriched form and continued to develop reaching a new height in the Song Dynasty (A.D. 960 – A.D. 1279). This new form of poetry was originally written for singing and was set to local or foreign (Central and Western Asia – 'barbarian' as was called) folk music. In order to fit the words into melodies, lyrics were therefore made up of long and short lines and with varying rhymes and beats. They were therefore markedly different from traditional Tang poems.

This new form of poetry was well received and became popular among intellectuals, officials and nobilities partly because it expressed subtle feelings more effectively and partly because listeners were fascinated and thrilled by the music, especially the vibrant Central and Western Asian music. They were therefore often sung at banquets and pleasure houses.

Among the six lyrics included in this Appendix, the two entitled "Breaking through the Ranks" (破陣子) and "Fair Lady Yu" (虞美人) by Li Yu (李煜) are legendary. The former is also one of the six model classical Chinese lyrics (詞範文) for the Hong Kong Diploma of Secondary Education Examination (DSE). Li Yu (李煜), better known as Li Houzhu (李後主), was a tragic figure. He was the last king of the Southern Tang (南 唐) and an outstanding poet. His lyrics are beautiful and overflowing with emotions. In these two touching lyrics, he unreservedly shared with readers his great sorrows after losing his kingdom.

The other four lyrics are chosen from well-known works of three great poets of the Tang and Song Dynasties namely: Ou-yang Xiu (歐陽修) who was also a famous statesman, historian and prose writer; Lu You (陸 游), a patriotic poet mentioned in the second paragraph above whose "Phoenix Hairpin" (釵頭鳳) tells his own touching tragic love story followed by "The Song of Divination" (卜算子) in which he used the fate of plum blossoms as an allusion to his unswerving integrity; Lin Bu (林逋) who is well-known for his romantic lyric poems.

附錄

宋詩兩首及唐宋詞六首

本書附錄兩首宋詩及六首唐宋詞，其目的在於引起讀者對宋詩及唐宋詞的興趣。在欣賞本書內的 202 首英譯唐詩之餘，也許你會喜愛同樣優美的宋詩及唐宋詞。

附錄內的兩首宋詩是南宋 (A.D. 1127 — A.D. 1279) 著名愛國詩人陸游的作品。陸游主張向入侵的金人發動全面戰爭，以奪回北方領土，但不為朝廷所接納並因而罷官。他留下 9,400 首詩及詞，堪稱古代最多產的詩人。第一首是他緬懷昔日邂逅其夫人而作，而第二首乃他 85 歲臨終時給兒子寫的遺言詩。可見他依然未忘光復國土。

唐宋詞起源於中唐至晚唐，以嶄新及更豐富的形式不斷發展，至宋朝 (A.D. 960 — A.D. 1279) 臻完美。此種新詩體原本是為本地或外地（中、西亞或稱蠻族）民歌的固定樂譜所配的曲詞，而所據的樂曲則稱為"詞牌"。為了要與原曲的旋律吻合，唐宋詞採用長短句及多變化的韻律與節奏，與傳統唐詩明顯不同。

此種新詩體在當時廣受文人雅士和達官貴人喜愛。其中原因是它能夠強而有力地表達細膩的感情，加上其所配的音樂（特別是中、西亞或稱蠻族的鏗鏘音樂）令聽曲者着迷。因而詞經常在宴會上及歡樂場所中，配以音樂唱出以娛賓客。

附錄內的六首詞之中，李煜的"破陣子"和"虞美人"是傳頌千古的佳作。"破陣子"亦被選為香港中學文憑試範文詞之一。李煜（即李後主）本人是一個悲劇角色。他是"南唐"一個軟弱國君，卻亦是個極出色的詩人。他的詞絢麗而洋溢着激情。在這兩首詞裏，他毫無保留地讓讀者感受到他那亡國之巨大悲痛。

　　其他四首詞分別選自唐、宋時期的三位偉大詩人的著名作品。 依次是歐陽修 —— 他亦是著名政治家、歷史學家及文學家；本文第二段所提及的陸游 —— 在"釵頭鳳"詞內，他細訴自己的愛情悲劇，在"卜算子"詞內，他以梅花隱喻自己對國家永恆的忠貞；最後是介紹精於寫浪漫曲子詞的林逋的作品。

SONG POEMS
宋詩

SPRING IN SHEN'S GARDEN

Lu You (1125 — 1210)

沈園春

陸游 (1125 — 1210)

The sun slants over the city wall
    amid the sad blare of the painted horn[1];
In Shen's Garden,
    old ponds and pavilions are all gone.

Under the heart-breaking bridge,
    green are the spring ripples
That once mirrored your elegant
    but transient image as you came along.

城上斜陽畫角哀，
沈園無復舊池臺。

傷心橋下春波綠，
曾是驚鴻照映來。

---

1 A horn (with pictures painted on it) was blown to signal time in ancient days. The poet was saddened
   by its sound as it reminded him of his past.

Background:
Lu You wrote this poem in A.D.1199 when he returned to Shen's Garden 40 years after he met his ex-
wife and wrote the famous lyric "Phoenix Hairpin" (釵頭鳳) on the garden wall.

TESTAMENT TO MY SON

Lu You (1125 — 1210)

示兒

陸游 (1125 — 1210)

With death I know everything will go:
Yet how sad witnessing of reunification
　　　of the nine provinces[1] I've to forgo.

On the day the Imperial troops
　　　recapture the North,
Forget not, in the family rite,
　　　to let your father know.

死去原知萬事空，
但悲不見九州同。

王師北定中原日，
家祭毋忘告乃翁。

1　In ancient times, China was divided into nine provinces. In the Southern Song Dynasty (A.D. 1127 —
　A.D. 1279), the Empire was truncated after the North provinces fell under the rule of the Jurgens i.e.
　the Jins (女真族即金人).

Background:
The poet was a senior official who had fought many battles against the invaders. He advocated launching
a full-scale fight-back to recapture the North but his proposition was not accepted. This poem was
written at his dying bed at the age of 85 and with great regret. He is revered as a patriotic poet.

TANG & SONG LYRICS
唐宋詞

BREAKING THROUGH THE RANKS

Li Yu (937 — 978)

For forty years,
    it's been my home and kingdom[1]
Extending three thousand li's[2],
    is the land my domain I call.

Phoenix pavilions and dragon towers
    rise to the sky;
Trees and flowers of jade hold me in thrall[3].

Do I ever know warfare at all?

Once taken prisoner[4],
My hair's turned grey, my waist small.

Most unforgettable was the day of
    my hasty and fearful departure from the shrine
While farewell songs
    were being played in the music hall.

Before the palace maids, I let my tears fall.

---

1 The kingdom of South Tang (南唐) was established in A.D. 937 by Li Sheng (李昇) and was overthrown during the poet's reign in A.D. 975. The kingdom lasted for a period of 38 years.

2 One Chinese li equals about 0.3 mile.

3 He was held in the thrall of his own super-luxurious life in the palace like someone being entangled by vines in the hills.

4 Li Yu (the poet and the last king of South Tang) was taken prisoner upon surrender to the Song army in A.D. 975 and was poisoned to death by order of the Song Emperor (宋太宗) on the 7th day of the 7th month in A.D. 978.

破陣子

李煜 (937 — 978)

四十年來家國，
三千里地山河。

鳳閣龍樓連霄漢，
玉樹瓊枝作煙蘿。

幾曾識干戈？

一旦歸為臣虜，
沉腰潘鬢消磨。

最是倉皇辭廟日，
教坊猶奏別離歌。

垂淚對宮娥。

FAIR LADY YU

Li Yu (937 — 978)

Spring flowers and autumn moon
    till when will they last?
How much do I know of things of the past?

To the small chamber,
    again came the east wind last night;

How unbearable to recall
    my lost kingdom in the moonlight!

Carved balustrades and jade steps
    should still be there,
But she no longer looks fair.

Do you know how much sorrow there is?
Just like a river of spring flowing east!

Background:
The poet was granted death by poison at the age of 42 not long after he composed this lyric which was believed to have upset the Song Emperor. He composed this and many other lyrics during the three years in captivity. He could not cast away his memories of a lost kingdom. He wished there were no more flowers and silvery moon to remind him of the happy days in his own palace.

虞美人

李煜（937 — 978）

春花秋月何時了，往事知多少？

　　小樓昨夜又東風，
　　故國不堪回首月明中。

雕闌玉砌應猶在，只是朱顏改。

　　問君能有幾多愁，
　　恰似一江春水向東流！

HAWTHORN

Ouyang Xiu (1007 — 1072)

Last year on Lantern Festival[1] night,
Lanterns in the flower fair bright as daylight.

The moon rose above the willows:
We dated in the twilight.

This year on Lantern Festival night,
The moon and lanterns remain bright.

My love of last year is nowhere to be found:
Tears wetted my spring sleeves outright.

---

1 Lantern Festival is also known as the Chinese lovers' day. It falls on the 15th day of 1st month in the
  lunar calendar, i.e. the first full moon night in the new year.

生查子

歐陽修（1007 — 1072）

去年元夜時，花市燈如晝。
月上柳梢頭，人約黃昏後。

今年元夜時，月與燈依舊，
不見去年人，淚濕春衫袖。

PHOENIX HAIRPIN

Lu You (1125 — 1210)

Hands pink and fine;
Yellow-seal wine[1].

Spring's colours fill the town but the willow's[2]
      trapped within the palace confines.

The east wind[3] was overly strong:
Our happiness didn't last long.

Separated for years,
A gloomy spirit all along.
Wrong! Wrong! Wrong!

Spring's the same as previous years,
But haggard your face appears:

Your silk handkerchief's soaked with rouged tears.

Peach blossoms fall,
Desolate the ponds and pavilions grow.

Our oath of love firm as ever,
But brocade letters to you would never go.
No! No! No!

---

1 Precious fine wine in delicate jars bearing a yellowish royal seal.

2 The poet alluded to his wife who was now in another man's arms just like the willow that was confined within the palace walls.

3 The east wind was blamed for blowing off flowers. Here the poet alluded to his mother who forced him to divorce his wife.

釵頭鳳

陸游 (1125 — 1210)

紅酥手，黃縢酒，
滿城春色宮牆柳。

東風惡，歡情薄，
一懷愁緒，幾年離索。錯！錯！錯！

春如舊，人空瘦，
淚痕紅浥鮫綃透。

桃花落，閒池閣。
山盟雖在，錦書難托。莫！莫！莫！

Background:
This poem recorded a famous love tragedy in the Southern Song Dynasty. Lu You (A.D. 1125 — A.D. 1210) was a famous patriotic poet. He and his wife Tang Wan (唐琬), who was also a distinguished poet, were deeply in love. Unfortunately, Tang was not acceptable to Lu's mother. Lu divorced Tang on instruction of his mother.
They met again on a fine spring day nine years afterwards in Shen's Garden (沈園). Tang was touring the garden with her second husband with whose approval, Tang entertained Lu with fine yellow-seal official wine. In return, Lu wrote the above lyric on the garden wall. Tang replied with another equally if not more touching lyric of the same tune. Tang died of a broken heart not long thereafter.

SONG OF DIVINATION (Song of the Plum)

Lu You (1125 — 1210)

By a broken bridge outside a courier post,
In loneliness it blooms in nobody's domain.

Dusk has fallen while alone it grieves –
Battered by the wind and rain.

Vie bitterly with spring it'd not;
Allow the jealousy of other flowers it'd fain.

When fallen, its blossoms would become mud
        and crushed into dust [1] –
Only their fragrance would remain.

---

1 After they were run over by the couriers' carriages.

Background:
The poet used the fate of plum blossoms as an allusion to his
unswerving integrity in the face of jealousy and vilification.

卜算子（詠梅）

陸游 (1125 — 1210)

驛外斷橋邊，
　寂寞開無主。

已是黃昏獨自愁，
　更着風和雨。

無意苦爭春，
　一任羣芳妒。

零落成泥碾作塵，
　只有香如故。

ETERNAL LONGING

Lin Bu (967 — 1028)

Mountains in Wu[1] are green;
Mountains in Yue[2] are also green.

Green mountains greet you
    on the banks in between.

Who knows what sentiments of parting mean?

With tears your eyes are dim;
With tears my eyes are also dim.

The chance of tying our love knots is slim.

Your boat's leaving
    now the tide has risen to the brim[3].

1&2 Small countries of feudal princes in the Zhou Dynasty by either side of the Qintong River around
    Zhejiang, Jiangsu and Anhui Provinces. Here the poet meant the mountains in the north and south.

3 When the tide rose to the brim, the water was deep enough for the boat to set sail.

長相思

林逋（967 — 1028）

吳山青，越山青，
兩岸青山相送迎。
誰知離別情？

君淚盈，妾淚盈，
羅帶同心結未成。
江頭潮已平。

Bibliography
參考書目

(1) *A Book of Chinese Verse*, by R. H. Kotewall & N. L. Smith, The Hong Kong University Press, Hong Kong, 1990.

(2) *A Golden Treasury of Chinese Poetry*, by John A. Turner, The Chinese University Press, Hong Kong, 1989.

(3) *A Silver Treasury of Chinese Lyrics*, edited by Alice W. Cheng, The Chinese University Press, Hong Kong, 2003.

(4) *Chinese Love Poetry*, edited by Jane Portal, British Museum Press, United Kingdom, 2004.

(5) *The 300 Tang Poems*, by Innes Herdan, the Far East Book Co. Ltd, Taipei, Taiwan, 2000.

(6) *Song Without Music, Chinese Tz'u Poetry*, edited by Stephen C. Soong, The Chinese University Press, Hong Kong, 1980.

(7) *A Brotherhood in Song, Chinese Poetry and Poetics*, edited by Stephen C. Soong, The Chinese University Press, Hong Kong, 1985.

(8) *Three Hundred Tang Poems*, by Peter Harris, published by Alfred A Knopf, 2009.

(9) *The Four Seasons of Tang Poetry* by John C. H. Wu, Charles E. Tuttle Company, Inc. of Rutland, Vermont & Tokyo Japan, 1972.

(10) *Selections from the Three Hundred Poems of Tang Dynasty* by Soame Jenyne, John Murray, London, 1944.

(11) *Three Chinese Poets, Translation of Poems* by Wang Wei, Li Bai and Du Fu by Vikram Seth, Harper Perennial, New York, 1993.

(12) *The Poetry of the Early Tang* by Stephen Owen, Yale University Press, New Haven, U.S.A., 1977.

(13) *The Great Age of Chinese Poetry: the High Tang* by Stephen Owen, Yale University Press, New Haven, USA, 1981.

(1) 《唐詩三百首》，蘅塘退士編選，香港萬里機構書店出版，2000 年。

(2) 《唐宋詞三百首》，蓋國梁編選，香港萬里機構書店出版，2000 年。

(3) 《唐詩三百首‧名家配畫誦讀本》，香港商務印書館出版，2000 年。

(4) 《唐宋詞三百首‧名家配畫誦讀本》，香港商務印書館出版，2000 年。

(5) 《唐詩三百首》，張芸主編，香港明報出版社出版，2005 年。

(6) 《新譯唐詩三百首》，邱燮友註譯，台灣三民書局印行，2007 年。

(7) 《新譯唐人絕句選》，卞孝萱，朱崇才註譯，台灣三民書局印行，2003 年。

(8) 《李白詩選，馬里千選註》，三聯書店（香港）有限公司出版，2012 年。

(9) 《杜甫詩選，梁鑒江選註》，三聯書店（香港）有限公司出版，2011 年。

(10) 《韓愈詩選，止水選註》，三聯書店（香港）有限公司出版，1998 年。

(11) 《中國文學史》，韓高年編著，台灣聯經出版事業股份有限公司出版，2011 年。

(12) 《唐宋名家詞選》，龍沐勛編選，卓清芬註說，台灣里仁書局發行，2007 年。

(13) 《唐宋名家詞選》，龍沐勛編選，香港商務印書館出版，1960 年。